TREASURE TRACKS

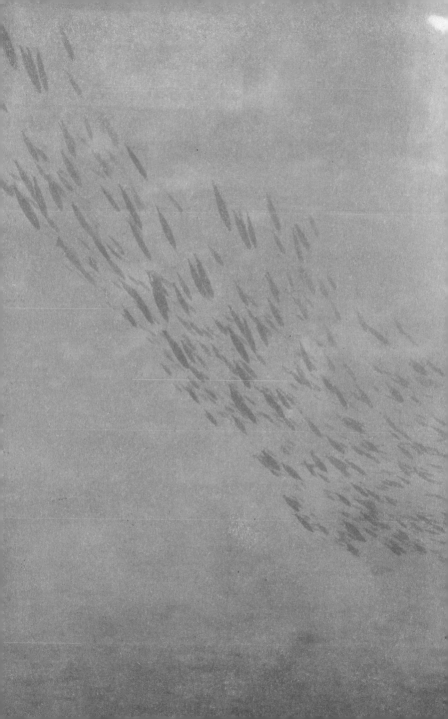

S.A. RODRIGUEZ

TREASURE TRACKS

SQUARE
FISH

FARRAR STRAUS GIROUX

NEW YORK

SQUARE
FISH

An imprint of Macmillan Publishing Group, LLC
120 Broadway, New York, NY 10271 • mackids.com

Square Fish and the Square Fish logo are trademarks of Macmillan and
are used by Farrar Straus Giroux under license from Macmillan.

Our books may be purchased in bulk for promotional, educational, or
business use. Please contact your local bookseller or the Macmillan
Corporate and Premium Sales Department at (800) 221-7945 ext. 5442 or
by email at MacmillanSpecialMarkets@macmillan.com.

The Library of Congress has cataloged the hardcover edition as follows:

Names: Rodriguez, Sallie Anne, author.
Title: Treasure tracks / Sallie Anne Rodriguez.
Description: First edition. | New York : Farrar Straus Giroux Books for
    Young Readers, 2022. | Audience: Ages 10–12. | Audience: Grades 4–6. |
    Summary: Twelve-year-old Fin drags his reluctant father on a diving hunt
    for a missing treasure, hoping that finding the family legacy will help his
    ailing abuelo.
Identifiers: LCCN 2021038642 | ISBN 9780374389796 (hardcover)
Subjects: CYAC: Buried treasure—Fiction. | Scuba diving—Fiction. |
    Hispanic Americans—Fiction. | Family life—Florida—Fiction. | Florida
    Keys (Fla.)—Fiction. | LCGFT: Novels.
Classification: LCC PZ7.1.R63958 Tr 2022 | DDC [Fic]—dc23
LC record available at https://lccn.loc.gov/2021038642

Originally published in the United States by Farrar Straus Giroux
First Square Fish edition, 2023
Book designed by Trisha Previte
Square Fish logo designed by Filomena Tuosto
Printed in the United States of America by Lakeside Book Company,
Harrisonburg, Virginia

ISBN 978-1-250-87865-6 (paperback)
10 9 8 7 6 5 4 3 2 1

AR: 6.0

For my mami in heaven

AUTHOR'S NOTE

Growing up in the Caribbean and Florida, I've been through my share of hurricanes. One stormy evening, I was hunkered down in Key Largo reading *Last Train to Paradise* by Les Standiford. It detailed the impacts of the Labor Day hurricane of 1935, the deadliest storm ever to hit the Florida Keys, and one of the strongest hurricanes ever recorded in history, with winds topping 185 miles per hour. Hundreds of souls were lost, including over two hundred World War I veterans stationed at relief work camps in the Middle Keys.

There were many tragic stories associated with this hurricane, which also caused railcars from Henry Flagler's Overseas Railroad, connecting Key West to the mainland, to be swept to sea. After it was destroyed, the railroad was never rebuilt, though some of its bridges and rails still stand, running parallel to the Overseas Highway. This got me thinking . . . How many stories from the passengers who perished on this train remained untold? And what if there was treasure on board?

Another devastating hurricane named Irma made landfall in the Florida Keys in September of 2017. I lived through this one and experienced its punishing blows. By combining the forces of this modern-day hurricane and the one from the past, *Treasure Tracks* came to life.

There are approximately one thousand documented shipwrecks in the waters surrounding the Florida Keys, many of them around Key Largo. Recognized as a diving capital of the world, the unique coral reef system in these waters is beautiful, but it can be deadly to ships because of the shallow waters and dangerous Gulf Stream current. And yes, hurricanes have done a lot of the sinking!

I have a personal passion for diving and underwater adventures. I dove Elbow Reef and the *City of Washington* wreck, the site featured on the cover, which inspired a climactic scene. I even had a close encounter with a blacktip shark at this spot and learned that if you leave sharks alone, they shouldn't bite.

Another thing I've learned: Adventures might be worth more than gold. So dive in, or at least dip your toes in the ocean.

TREASURE TRACKS

1
A PIRATE'S SOUL

Submerged in the deep blue ocean, the world stood still all around me. I'm talking *too* still, with fish and all the wonders of the sea in hiding mode. Only seagrass and sand.

Boring . . .

My first official creds-secured scuba dive and I'd discovered a big ol' nothing. Goose egg. Zero on the adventure scale.

Abuelo Kiki made frantic hand gestures beside me. *Up. Up. Up.*

A glance at the gauge confirmed my air would end soon. I propelled myself from the sandy bottom. Off like a rocket.

Swoosh.

Bubbles trailed behind. Within seconds, my face broke above the final wall of clear blue water, bathwater warm in the heat. The sky greeted us, but the early September sun was not smiling down. Dark gray clouds warned of trouble.

Abuelo surfaced next to me. "No time to lose, Fin. Weather's 'bout to turn. Some of the outer bands of the storm seem to be making their way in. Gotta shove on. Highway's gonna be crammed—everyone fighting to get out. And I promised to get you home to Miami before it hit."

"Wish we could stay and hang in the Keys," I grumbled.

"According to the weather radio this morning, Hurricane Irma's 'bout a hundred miles south of here, ravaging Cuba. She'll travel up the Florida Straits and hit us some time tomorrow morning."

I yanked off my mask and regulator. The challenge was balancing the heavy tank on my back. The duck-like fins on my feet didn't make it any easier. Waddle, waddle. My knees buckled in awkward angles climbing the ladder on the stern of the boat.

Abuelo plopped onto the deck behind me, his chest rising up and down in labored movements. He struggled to tear off gear. Gone was the rock-hard strength that used to pulse through his tanned arms. His faded anchor tattoo sagged where impressive lumps used to bulge on his biceps.

How could this be? He was so much tougher than me.

"Pass me your tank." I extended a hand.

"I can manage on my own," Abuelo snapped. "Get busy. Pull down the dive flag and bring up the anchor." He gestured to the bow of his vintage 1973 nineteen-foot Boston Whaler. "Don't know how I let you talk me into going out today."

"Birthday gift," I reminded him, before crawling along the rails, real grateful to have my sea legs back and lose the clumsy web feet.

I pulled on the line stretched out from a cleat on the bow but couldn't get the anchor to budge. Not one bit.

From the stern, Abuelo grunted in his usual drill-sergeant way. "Come on, boy. Give it some muscle."

My palms stung as I struggled to keep a grip on the wet line. I braced myself and pulled, inch by inch. No chance I'd let Abuelo down even if my pitiful pecs were still in training. Besides, one day soon, I'd help him haul up something way better than this stupid dead weight.

"Argh!" I finally lugged the anchor on board and waved an imaginary pirate hook in the air. "Not letting anyone mess with our treasure."

"Little to worry about," Abuelo scoffed. "No one knows it exists."

"But there're hundreds of divers coming out to the Florida Keys."

As if on cue, a boat motored into view with a CONCHER SCUBA logo painted on its side. The big C at the front curved into a sea serpent tail slithering under the rest of the letters.

"See what I mean? Invading."

"That there's a divemaster. One of the pros. Paid to be out, unlike me."

The driver saluted before racing out of sight.

"You think he's after our loot? Only other boat we've seen since we anchored here."

"Different kinds." Abuelo chuckled. "Treasure comes in many forms. Natural ones hidden all over our coral reefs."

"I want the real stuff . . ."

"Sure you do. Couldn't wait a day past your twelfth birthday to go hunting, aye, matey?" He winked.

Over the summer he had paid for my scuba lessons and given me equipment. I'd just finished the course and was now officially a Junior Open Water Scuba Diver. I knew the lessons and my equipment had cost him a lot, but he never grumbled about it.

I raised two thumbs in the air. "Been waiting to get certified for a looong time." Like, my whole life long. Or at least since the first time I remember dipping my toes in the ocean. A school of minnows came to greet me. We played hide-and-seek, but Mami had to grab me when I tried to follow them into the deep.

Abuelo's expression turned serious, pulling me out of memory-mode. "You got no business having me as your dive buddy. I'm getting too old for this."

"Old?" I snorted. "You act younger than Dad." Way, way younger. "Where's your sense of adventure? It's what you always tell him."

Abuelo took my bait. "Listen, squirt. Back in my day, I could teach you a thing or two about diving and adventure." He shook his finger and his voice dropped to a whisper. "But your dad will have my head mounted on a wall like my sailfish if he gets wind of what we're up to. Too risky as far as he'd be concerned. Especially with the storm on the way."

"Relax . . . You always say I practically have gills. It'll be our secret." I drew a finger to my lips. "As usual."

"I know all too well about them gills of yours. Ya got salt water flowing through your veins. How you think you landed your nickname, Fin?"

I rolled my eyes, even though I was totally grateful for the nickname he'd given me. Fin was way cooler than the über-Latino name my parents—or actually, Mami—gave me: *Fernando*. If I closed my eyes, I could hear Mami belting out Lady Gaga's song "Alejandro." Mami's version was heavy on the Spanish accent and super exaggerated rolling of the R's. Especially the part where she'd scream out my name when the refrain switched to "Ferrrrnando!"

Ugh. Made my skin crawl.

Abuelo interrupted my thoughts. "You were two years old. Even then you used to jump and swim out from my dock. No one could stop you. Used to scare the bejesus out of your dad. Think you learned to swim before you could walk. Born with fins, I always said."

I gave him my best cheeky grin. "Yep, meant to be diving. Besides, only forty feet deep here. Not risky at all. We didn't even have to stop and decompress. How much trouble could we possibly get into?"

BOOM!

The distant cannon of a thunderbolt fired off a warning.

"Get into position," Abuelo commanded. I hustled back to sit next to him in the captain's chair, which was big enough for both of us.

He rummaged through his duffel bag and pulled out his favorite Panama hat. Pressing the straw covering over his head, he added shade to a splattering of sunspots. "Let's go batten down the hatches. Hit the road." He revved the 150 horses of his Evinrude outboard to life, shouting over the noise: "Not much time left, and this Irma gal's a mean one! She'll be packing quite a punch coming in as a Cat Four."

I gripped the handrail that went around the console. The boat slammed up and down, pounding over the waves, and swayed from side to side. Water splashed onto the deck, slapping sea salt over every inch of my skin. Dampening my courage. Gulp. "You really think Irma is going to be as bad as they say?" I shouted.

Abuelo frowned. "Who knows? But we haven't had a real monster hit the Keys since the Labor Day hurricane of 1935. Storm of the century, they called it."

"Were you there? For the storm of the century?"

"Hey." Abuelo jabbed lightly at my shoulder. "I'm getting old, but not that old."

Right. Duh. I did the math in my head. He'd have to be ancient, more than ninety, to remember that storm.

"Almost wiped out the Keys. Swept away our railroad."

A crackle of lightning hit the water near the port side of the boat.

As more thunder boomed, Abuelo studied the sky again. "Hold tight!" He put the engine into full throttle and strengthened his grip on the wheel.

I sank deeper into the seat cushions. "Too bad it's gone!"

"Not just lost. It went POOF!" He snapped his fingers. "Swallowed up by the sea. Tidal wave hit the train," he bellowed. "Flung all the railcars on their sides like toys."

A strong gust of wind whisked away his hat, but he didn't bother glancing over the stern, where it disappeared in our churning wake. Far beyond reach.

Me, I leaned into him in the captain's chair, holding on till my knuckles turned white.

Long minutes elapsed until we approached shore, passing a SLOW NO WAKE marker as Abuelo pulled way back on the throttle.

"The treasure," Abuelo said. "It was on board."

WHAT?

"You never told me about the train before. Only that you knew the way to a lost treasure. This is a way cooler story."

Abuelo's nod turned somber. He stared over the horizon. "'Bout time I tell you the truth. Don't think anyone else knows."

"Only me?" This was a big deal. He chose to trust me! "How do you know?" I pressed on. One thing was sure, Abuelo's life was part mystery.

He ignored my question. "I won't be around forever. This'll be your secret to keep."

"You know I'm a good keeper of secrets. We're co-conspirators, you always tell me." I tried my best to wink, though it probably looked more like an eye spasm as I did the one-eyed blinky-blink.

Abuelo smiled. "At least I got one trouper left in the family."

Yep, that's me. Team Abuelo and Fin.

"Get to the good stuff!" I urged, rubbing my sore hands together. "Do you know what's hidden in the chest?"

Abuelo fell silent, his eyes trained over the ocean as we sliced through angry swells.

"Don't stop," I pleaded.

The wind responded with a high-pitched howl and a punch to the side of the hull.

Abuelo started up again. "Never said it was buried in a chest. This isn't pirate treasure like in some bedtime story." He chuckled. "It's real. Old Spanish gold brought in from Cuba. Who knows where it came from. Probably an old shipwreck. Must be worth millions today."

Millions? This was far more than I ever imagined.

"It comes from the same place we do?"

"Yes. Your home country. At least from my side. You got your mom's Puerto Rican blood mixed in, too. *Frijoles con habichuelas.*" He snickered. "Mix of Caribbean beans."

Forget the beans. Images of glowing doubloons floated through my mind. "So, if it's gold, it kind of is like pirate treasure. They always had those old coins stashed in chests."

Abuelo shook his head as he turned into the narrow canal leading to his home. As we approached, he cut the motor, letting the boat drift up to his dock. The second it bumped against the edge, I jumped onto the wooden planks to complete my first-mate duties. I knotted a thick blue line to a metal cleat the way he'd taught me and I'd perfected.

"Grab a bumper." He pointed, then started attaching more lines to the boat and throwing them to me. "Gotta tie up real good before we scoot outta here. Make sure *Sirena* makes it. Canal should protect her from the bigger swells."

My mind was on other things as I secured the rubber fender toward the stern. "We'll find it. I know we can."

"I've tried for many years, you know. It's a treasure that doesn't want to be found. Still lies in a watery grave."

A shiver went up my spine. "You think when we find it there'll be creepy pirate skeletons watching over it?"

"You've got Captain Jack Sparrow on the brain, Fin, but lots of piracy in the Caribbean to be sure. They weren't the glorified adventurers you see in movies, though. Cuba built these huge fortresses to defend itself. Keep 'em out."

"Wish we could visit Cuba together." I'd love a chance to visit the place in person after all these years of listening to his stories. He'd taken me to Little Havana in Miami, named after the capital of Cuba, where we'd played dominoes in a park, but that couldn't possibly be the same thing.

"One day when it's free. Not giving a dime to those dictators." Abuelo's voice trembled with anger till it shook up a fit of coughing.

"Right." Useless try. Best not to get Abuelo started. I had his Cuban rants practically memorized. Besides, I liked my American freedoms just so. "We'll be so rich when we find it, we can go anywhere."

"Careful, Fin. Treasure can turn men into real pirates," Abuelo mumbled.

Another bolt of lightning shot down from the heavens to match the warning in his tone. In spite of the heat and humidity, a chill crept all the way down to my bones.

2
TWISTED REALITY

Less than an hour later, I plopped into the cab of Abuelo's pickup. We rolled up the Overseas Highway, the famous interstate cutting through the sea, with bridge after bridge connecting the long string of small islands known as keys. It was supposed to deliver the sweeping water views printed on countless postcards that said *Greetings from the Florida Keys! Wish You Were Here!* Except now the highway offered the exact opposite of a welcome.

Waves threatened to drown out the road as the surf crept its way in. And for sure, Abuelo's truck wouldn't be able to swim nearly as well as me. Even the palm trees warned things were anything but the usual serene. Their leaves made an angry dance in the heavy breeze.

Inches ahead, an eighteen-wheeler rattled to a dead

stop, blasting out a cloud of black smoke that drifted back through our windows, filling my lungs.

Cough. Cough.

"Crapola," Abuelo muttered. "I was hoping to beat the rush. Parking lot out here now. At this rate, we won't reach Miami till nightfall. And this toxic—"

Ding ding ding. My phone had been working fine yesterday when Abuelo and I left the mainland and came down to his place, but there'd been no service all morning. Until now. Maybe something to do with the storm.

"You gonna answer those beeps? I'm getting ready to throw that darned phone of yours out the window. Not sure why you young people even bother with those things. All this technology stuff telling you what to do. Always on. Always intruding."

My phone now displayed five missed calls and eight messages:

Mami (8:03 a.m.): Happy birthday! See U soon. ☺

Mami (12:17 p.m.): Where are U? Supposed to be home hours ago.

Mami (1:30 p.m.): Call me.

Mami (2:40 p.m.): Call me. Now!

Mami (3:22 p.m.): You better call me right NOW!

Dad (3:35 p.m.): Report home. We're worried.

Mami (3:47 p.m.): Hurricane is hitting soon. Are U OK?

Mami (3:52 p.m.): Will call police to search for U.

I took a deep breath (*cough, cough*) before pressing the phone symbol in her contact. Good thing she couldn't wring my neck over the airwaves.

Mami answered on the first ring. "Fernando Javier Cordero Román, where have you been?" she yelled.

Ouch. If she was torturing me with my full-on Latino name—all four ridiculous parts of it—she had to be a ten out of ten on the anger scale. I pulled the cell farther from my ear. "What's up? Why you texting like a hundred times? I'm okay."

"What is up? Really? Why didn't you call sooner? I got you the phone so we could keep tabs on you!"

"My phone hasn't been getting service until just now. I swear. We're driving back now. Promise. Traffic's bad."

"Oh, okay. And happy birthday, *mi amor*." Bitter melted to sugar sweet in Mami's still-too-loud voice. "When will you be home?"

I glanced at Abuelo. "Could be hours," he said with a shrug.

"No clue, Mami."

"Did I hear Enrique say hours? Hours! ¡*Por Dios!*"
Her cry turned to silence—a standard extra helping of
mom guilt. What did I even do?

I stared at the phone. "She hung up."

"That didn't go so well," Abuelo said with a smirk.
"Sure I'll get an earful, too. Promised I'd get you back
way before the storm hit, and we might be losing the
race." He popped his head out the driver's window to
stare at the dark sky.

"You mean the hurricane's going to hit us in your
truck?" I tried to stay calm, but a wall of angry black
clouds choked out the light, strangling my cool.

"Nah." As the music station we were listening to cut to
commercials, Abuelo messed around with the dial. He
stopped when he reached a news channel.

We sat in silence for the next few minutes listening
to the weatherman go on and on. A never-ending list of
predictions and warnings that all said the same thing:
"Alert. Alert. Run for your lives!"

"Not sure how I'm going to make it back to the Keys
tonight before they shut it down," Abuelo grumbled
before switching over to a music station.

"What do you mean? You're not staying with us? The weather dude said the Keys could get wiped away with the tidal surge."

"Nothing's going to wash away this old man."

Old?

I turned to look at him as he peered out the windshield. Deep wrinkles were set at the corners of Abuelo's eyes, and for the first time, I noticed his thin gray hair had turned a silvery shade of white. When did that happen?

"Rather keep *Sirena* company. Make sure my girl doesn't sink. Don't need another treasure swallowed up by the sea. 'Sides, you know your dad and I don't do well in the same room for too long."

"But, but . . . you can't—" I pouted. Could it be he loved his boat more than his favorite grandson? His only grandson. Me? His *Sirena* shouldn't be reason enough to stay. I grasped at a way to keep him with me. "You could get washed out like the railroad did."

"Save it, boy. Times were different back then. My house is solid concrete on stilts. Even has those shutters we bolted on at the crack of dawn."

"What if something happened to you?"

"The important thing is I get you home safe. You got your whole life ahead of you. I've already had my share of adventures."

My heart skipped a beat. "Don't talk like that! You freak me out when you do."

Abuelo smiled, but terrible thoughts invaded my head. I couldn't get past the image of the train getting swept over by the sea. "Do you have any idea where the treasure went? Is it where we dove today?"

"Happened so long ago, currents could have taken it anywhere. Buried it deep. Could be miles and miles out to sea from where the train went off the tracks. We're looking for a needle in an endless ocean haystack."

"You mean you don't have actual coordinates—GPS stuff? I always thought you had a hidden treasure map with spots to check out."

"Nope, educated guesses are better than tech any day. Been studying these waters for years." Abuelo chuckled. "But did you know that this highway follows some of the exact same path where the railroad tracks used to be?"

"No way!" I said. As I looked out at the churning surf, my worries about getting swept away by the stormy sea only got worse.

Pop. Pop. Pop. Tiny ice bullets sounded off like party

poppers slamming against the driveway on a Fourth of July. They pelted the roof and windshield with pint-sized fury. I stared out the window and couldn't believe what I saw.

"What . . . what . . . what's that?" My finger shook, pointing to a thin funnel dropping down from a cloud. It sucked up water with every rotation twirling its way over the ocean. Toward us. "Is that part of the hurricane? A to—tornado?"

Images of Abuelo's truck getting scooped up and spit out in an imaginary Oz-land terrorized my thoughts. Instead of the Wicked Witch of the West, I'd end up in the lost kingdom of Atlantis face-to-face with a giant man-eating squid. I'd hated squids ever since dissecting one in science class. I closed my eyes as I imagined his evil tentacles bedazzled in red rubies lunging at me.

Ahhh! Why'd I even watch all those crazy movies?

I slapped myself straight across the face. *Stop*.

"*Tranquilo*, Fin." Abuelo put his hand over mine. "It's only a small waterspout. They hardly ever make their way inland. We get them all the time. No big deal."

Yeah, right. No. Big. Deal.

"More waterspouts in the Keys than anywhere in the world."

"That's supposed to make me feel better?" I sucked in my breath and put on my bravest face. It's what Abuelo would expect. "Fearless Fin, Fearless Fin," I chanted under my breath, summoning the courage of the two-year-old version of me he had described.

No use. Only swimming in the ocean made me fearless. We were suspended above it—high as a skyscraper. On the tippy top hump of a bridge. "Will . . . will we get blown off if it hits us? We're not exactly inland."

"Nah, stop worrying."

"But we're stuck up here. Like. Not. Moving. And your truck's rocking back and forth."

"A little rain and wind. Lots worse than this to come. Look." Abuelo pointed. "Traffic's starting to move. We'll roll off in no time, and spout's almost gone. They don't last long."

At least that part was true. Only a thin line shooting down from the wall cloud remained while we inched our way forward.

Just when I was feeling a little safer, he said, "Keep your eyes peeled for crocodiles now." Abuelo waggled his eyebrows and pointed to a CROCODILE CROSSING sign on the side of the road. "Long stretch of Everglades to go before we hit the concrete jungle."

"Very funny. I'm sure they're all hiding. Even the fish were out of sight when we dove."

"Birds are gone, too. Animals sense the big storms way before our sophisticated instruments do—"

Blaring sirens and a loud buzzing sound shut out all other noise. A line of police cars raced south on the opposite side of the highway. A helicopter followed the convoy, keeping close to the ground, away from the clouds and near the action.

I could make out a news station logo at the same time a man leaned through the open door. He balanced a video camera in his arms and jerked it in our direction. We were part of the news!

"Hey!" I stuck my head out the truck window and made the radical sign with both hands. "What's with all the cops?" I turned to Abuelo.

A flush of frustration crept across his face. "Looks like they're doing a final sweep. I guess they are closing off all the highway going into the Keys. You can get out, but you can't go back in. Better if it were more like this 'Hotel California' tune." Abuelo cranked up the radio. "'You can check out any time you like, but you can never leave!'" he sang along. "Much better never leaving the island side."

I ignored his grumbling and fist-pumped the air. "Sorry to make you ditch the Keys for me, but it means you get to check in at my house. 'And never leave!'" Hee-hee. "You can't go back tonight."

"Great . . ." Abuelo snorted.

Eventually, we crossed the last stretch of mangroves and were finally on the mainland.

The instant his pickup swerved into the driveway of my house, Mami's face peeked out behind silk curtains by the front window. She ran outside with our Chihuahua, Ratón, in her arms, and yanked open my door. "Fernando! *Por fin.*"

I tumbled out of the truck and into her arms, drowning in the aroma of her violet-scented floral perfume and dog breath. "Geez, Mami, it's only been two days."

"*¿Estás bien?* You had me so worried." She looked me up and down. "You hanging out in the ocean so much, you're getting blond streaks in your hair. The first *rubio* in the family."

I stepped back—enough to breathe violet-free air. At

least she was in a better mood. "All good. We saw a tornado. But it didn't hit us."

"A tornad-O?" Mami's eyes and red-lipsticked mouth opened wide.

Abuelo grinned. "More like a small waterspout way out over the ocean. Storm's moving in quick—"

"And Abuelo has to stay with us. They closed the highway."

"*Entra*, Enrique, you know you're always welcome." Mami ushered us toward the door. "We'll get you settled."

Dad caught up to us on the front porch. He wore a yellow construction hat and safety goggles in place of his usual eyeglasses. A leather toolbelt hung around the bulge in his waist, and he held a new wireless electric drill in his right hand loaded with a screwdriver bit. "You took your time getting our son home." Annoyance dripped off him along with beads of sweat.

"It's not Abuelo's fault," I said. Why did Dad always have to go at him?

"You have any idea what traffic's like?" his father snapped, color rising to his face again.

"Hmpff. Could've used a hand here, Fernando. Your

mom and I already moved all the outdoor furniture in. Only need to finish putting up two more shutters."

Dad was trying to shame me in his usual way, using his sour mood as an excuse to call attention to the little things I'd done wrong in his eyes.

Abuelo smirked, jumping in. "Yes, I see you've been busy. Even exchanged your suit for a Bob the Builder getup."

Hee-hee. Nailed it!

Dad locked eyes with him. Only seconds had passed, and he and Abuelo had already declared war.

"How about we go in and get you boys something cold to drink?" Mami the peacemaker swept in.

"I can do the last two shutters," I offered.

"You're too young to be using a power tool."

"What do you mean? I used Abuelo's this morning. And I'm twelve. Like, today, remember? Stop treating me like a baby. I can do more than move lawn chairs."

Dad scowled at Abuelo before giving me a half-smile. "Happy birthday, son."

"Glad he could remind you," Abuelo said.

"Sorry, but in case you didn't notice we're operating under a state of emergency."

"No biggie," I said. Now it was my turn to play

peacemaker. "At least you and Mami let me stay with Abuelo. He gave me the coolest present. My scuba certification. It's the best birthday ever."

"Fernando, we didn't forget your big day. We got you a cake and candles to blow," said Mami.

"You mean you'll sing me your Puerto Rican birthday anthem? The Amiguito song?" I made a face and stuck out my tongue.

"Come on. It's sweet," Mami said. "Let's get out of this heat. We'll do the cake once your dad is done blowing all his hot air out." She concealed a grin.

Dad shot Abuelo and Mami a look. Easy to read: *I am not happy.* "Going back to finishing the shutters," he huffed.

Abuelo rolled his eyes. "Let's go inside, Fin. Your father has this all under control. As usual. This should be a fun couple of days riding out the storm," he muttered under his breath.

"You got that right," Dad said as he walked away. "It'll be a jolly good time . . ."

I cringed. Because only Dad would use a corny word like *jolly.*

3
LIGHT UP THE SAINTS

Within hours, the worst part of the storm arrived. The four of us packed ourselves in the windowless laundry room: Mami, Dad, Ratón, and me.

"Safest room in the house," Dad said after chasing us into the closet-sized space with barely an inch left to breathe.

The air smelled like a toxic floral mix of detergent, fabric softener, and dryer sheets. After a while I propped the door open to let in some fresh air and peek out. "No fair. How come Abuelo gets to hang in the family room watching TV?"

Tyrant Dad needed a big dose of Abuelo's chill.

Ratón barked in agreement.

"Can I go out with him?" I begged.

Woof.

"*¡Ya, silencio!*" Mami yelled at Ratón.

Ratón looked up at her with sad, droopy eyes.

Mami blew air kisses. "I still love you." Her voice squeaked in high-pitched baby speak. "Yes. Yes. *Perdona, mi ratoncito.*"

Arf! Arf! Arf!

"No, stay put, Fin. You cannot go out. It's not safe," Dad shouted over the barking. He turned to Mami. "Let the darned dog out. He's driving me crazy."

"But you said it's not . . . safe." Mami narrowed her eyes. "Why would you put Ratón's life at risk?"

"Because he won't shut up. He can go hang with my dad."

Mami put a possessive arm around the dog. "If Ratón goes, I go too—"

CRACK! Thunder exploded, and the whole room shook. The ceiling light flickered—on, off, on.

Off.

Yikes! Darkness ended up being the choice, drowning us in a pit of flowery oblivion.

"Ahh!" Mami screamed. "*Ya empezó.*"

"The high winds are moving in." Dad snapped on the flashlight he had tucked next to him and placed it under his face, so he lit up white as a ghost.

Ratón pawed at me, digging his sharp nails into my skin. His woofs had turned to whimpers.

"You hear the wind howling?" Dad put his hand over Mami's.

I wanted to howl, too. Get me out of here!

"*Ilumíname,*" Mami said, directing Dad's light toward her candles. She struck a match, bringing all five of her tall votives to life. Each displayed a different virgin or saint. And if you gave her an hour, she'd explain how each offered a different path to guide us to salvation. She made the sign of the cross and brought her hands together in prayer.

Me, I prayed to break free from this hole. Abuelo had a way better setup.

"Don't worry. We'll get through this together." Dad snapped off the flashlight now that the candles were lit.

I cracked open the door again. "Abuelo, you wanna join us?" Hee-hee. He'd laugh at my joke.

Ratón dashed out, knocking over one of Mami's *santos.*

"*¡Mi bebé!*" Mami yelled.

"Now look what you've done." Dad flicked on the spotlight so it shone on my face. Guilty.

I covered my eyes. "A minute ago you wanted Ratón out. I did you a favor."

"But of course I didn't mean it." He grinned at Mami.

Abuelo approached with Mami's favorite votive illuminating his path. This one displayed the Virgin adorned with a fancy crown of gold and baby Jesus in her arms. Mami's spoiled baby squirmed in his free hand. "Here's your little yapper. Good thing you got these lying all over the house, Carmen." He raised the holy candle.

"The saints will protect us." Mami cradled Ratón back in her arms. "Especially the one you're holding. It's the Virgen de la Caridad del Cobre, the patron saint of your country. She represents hope and salvation."

"Something all Cubans need," Abuelo admitted.

"Legend has it Our Lady of Charity led to the rescue of two indigenous Cubans and a ten-year-old enslaved boy caught in a storm at sea back in the early 1600s. She was also believed to have guided the freeing of enslaved Cubans by the king of Spain, two hundred years later. Freed them from oppression in copper mines—it's where the 'cobre' part of the name originated." Mami patted the hard tiles. "Come and join us. I'll tell you more."

"Seriously, Mami? You're going to give us a religion lesson?"

"Sorry, would love to hear all about Cuban salvation, but not a chance I'm getting caught in your can of sardines. With no electricity, it's the perfect time to sleep." Abuelo turned on his heels. "If your Lady of Charity doesn't come through for you in this storm, you can wake me if the roof blows."

"You have to say that in front of . . . ?" Dad called after him.

I knew he was referring to me. "It's okay. I'm not scared." True, I was a little scared of the waterspout I'd seen earlier, but not now, hiding next to our washer and dryer and Mami's group of saints.

"Well, you should be!" Dad said. With perfect timing, thunder crashed above. "Hurricanes are to be taken seriously."

Okay, correction. Maybe I was a tad bit scared . . .

"I'll pray for you," Mami called after Abuelo, making the sign of the cross again.

Dad locked the door and blocked the entrance with his body as if his weight alone could keep the storm from barging in. He projected a circle of light across the walls and ceiling, casting shadows, creepy and tall. I sat in silence watching them dance and twirl—round and round.

With each passing minute, the air hung heavier as the hurricane pressed down with a giant lead hand. This would be the barometric pressure drop—lowest near the center of the storm. I imagined it like the pressurized air inside my dive tank. But yikes, could it really be so? We were nearing the eye of the storm, which meant we were only halfway through receiving its punishing blows.

Ratón let out a human-sounding yelp. His tiny pointed ears drooped and his body trembled. I sucked in my breath, regulating my air as I would on the ocean bottom. I needed to stay calmer than the dog.

"Starting to sound like a train going over our roof," Dad exclaimed. "This might be the worst part before we get a break when the eye passes over us."

Mami's voice cracked. "Victor, that's not helping."

Nope. Not at all . . . I had to change the subject, take my mind off the evil eye closing in full force.

"Abuelo mentioned a train got smashed by a hurricane in the Keys a long time ago."

"You mean what's referred to as Flagler's folly back in the thirties?" Dad placed the flashlight under his chin again, so his face was all aglow. "Did you know his father worked with the railroad at the time? My abuelo."

Really? "He didn't mention that part."

"I never had a chance to meet him. Passed away before I was born. In fact, he died at sea. Still don't know how I let you talk me into going down to the Keys yesterday. Even missing a day of school. Shouldn't be diving. Way too dangerous."

"Abuelo didn't tell me that's how he . . . died."

"Of course not. Just like him to leave out the important details. Should make you take pause. Choose a safer sport."

"Wouldn't be fun. Down deep, I get to float free like the fish. Visit their world. Explore—"

BOOOOOM!

It seemed like a bomb exploded overhead, shaking the house to its core.

"*¡Ay, Dios mío!*" Mami screamed. "Whatever fell on us was huge."

"Will the house cave in?" I squeaked. "That felt more like an earthquake."

Dad stared at the ceiling, worry lines creasing his forehead. "All I know is we're staying put until this all passes. Could be hours before Irma blows through."

Mami grabbed hold of a saint candle and raised it to study the walls. The color had drained from her face, so she looked like a red-lipped ghost.

And seriously, why was she even wearing lipstick?

"Don't worry." Dad pulled Mami into his shoulder and kissed the top of her head. "We're in an interior room. No windows. Safest place to be. I suggest we all try getting some rest." He stood and tossed blankets and pillows from a stack atop the dryer. "Prop yourself up to sleep."

"Are you kidding? There's no room to move," I grumbled. "And it's scorching hot with the AC off." I threw back the blanket.

"Best we can do." He snapped off the light and bent to blow out Mami's candles.

The wind intensified to a howling scream.

With nothing but pitch dark, my eyes were useless, but my ears snapped to high alert with every creak.

At last, the lights went out in my head, too, and I slept.

4
INCOMMUNICADO

The next morning, Mami and I made our way out of our shelter after Dad gave the all-clear.

"Ay, ay, ay," Mami shrieked. "*¡Mira!*" She slapped a palm over her forehead. Long red fingernails pointed out to match the smudges left on her lips.

I followed her stare. Shoot! A tree lay smack in the center of the family room. Its leaves lay scattered all over the floor, spritzing the room with forest-scented deodorizer. Unwelcome perfume.

How did I sleep through this?

"*Dios mío*, you can see sky." Her bottom lip quivered. Tears welled up in her eyes, causing eyeliner to run down in streaks.

"It's okay." I hugged Mami the way she would do to

me. Somehow it always managed to make me feel a little better. "It can get fixed."

I think.

The limbs, piled high over the couch, told a different story. They tangled together, looking like a mass of shattered bones protruding in all sorts of awkward directions. In the exact spot where Abuelo sat and watched TV last night.

Abuelo!

My heart thumped. I raced toward the guest room and tried turning the knob on his door.

Locked.

"Abuelo, open up. You okay?" I banged until my knuckles throbbed.

"Answer me. Please."

Silence.

I darted to my bedroom and rummaged through the desk. Think like a thief. I could pop the lock with the right kind of tool.

I settled on a pen and snapped it open. The ink cartridge would be thin enough to fit through the tiny hole in the door handle.

Emergency key in hand, I ran back to operate on the

door, jamming the cartridge round and round, till *click*. Genius. It opened on my command.

"Abuelo! Abuelo!" I ran to his side and shook his body.

His chest moved in a steady rhythm. Up. Down. Up. Down.

"Wake up!"

His eyes pried open, and he stretched his arms wide, mouth open in a big yawn. "What's with all the fuss?"

Phew.

"The hurricane passed."

Abuelo yawned again before draping his legs over the side of the bed in a lazy motion. "Good riddance, Irma."

"Why'd you lock yourself in? You scared me."

"Trying to keep the hurricane out, Fin." He chuckled. "Took a big sleeping pill and didn't hear a thing. Best way to ride out the storm and block out Ratón. How'd you all do? The house?"

"Not good. Come look."

"*Buenos días.*" Mami greeted Abuelo with a half-hearted smile. Her eyeliner had painted dark blotches around her eyes, so she looked more racoonish than human. "Did you sleep okay?"

Dad joined us in the family room, notepad and pencil in hand. *Tap. Tap. Tap.* "I've completed a full assessment. Roof's a wreck. Yard and pool a mess—darned thing looks like a green swamp. Perimeter light—"

"Stop." Abuelo put his hands over his ears. "I just rolled out of bed. Way too early for one of your checklists."

Dad ignored him and kept right on tapping. "Lots to do, and we may not have electricity restored for days. Even weeks."

"*Ay, bendito*, I couldn't even make us *cafecito*." Mami wrung her hands together in a tortured rhythm.

Abuelo grimaced. "Now that is bad news." He stared at the gaping hole in the ceiling. "I see you got a new skylight."

"Not funny," Dad shot back. "Not time for one of your jokes."

For once, I agreed. The big hole made Mami cry, which wasn't something she often did. I tried to break the tension. "Things could be worse. We're all good."

"Victor," Mami scolded her husband. "No fighting. Fernando is right. The important thing is we're alive."

Ratón barked and ran up to her, tail wagging and long pink tongue hanging out.

"Yes, yes, I know you're alive, too," she whispered.

"At least we have insurance to cover damages," Dad said.

"Of course you do," Abuelo said sarcastically, refusing to give Dad a break. "Any update on the Keys?" he asked. "Last night, the meteorologist on the news predicted the hurricane would blast right through."

"We don't have power. Wi-Fi. Anything. Cut off from the world and all news. Hard to say what's happened. Can't even drive down the street until they clear all the fallen trees and debris. Could be holed up for days," Dad said with a sigh.

Abuelo groaned. "Gotta check on my house," he said. He grabbed his car keys and headed toward the front door.

We followed him to the door. Outside, the sky was bright blue, and a gentle breeze was blowing.

"Did you hear the part about roads being blocked with debris?" Dad shouted after him. "I'm sure the Overseas Highway is still closed. You can't leave."

I had to side with Dad again. "Please, Abuelo. Hang with us. Don't leave."

"Relax. The tree didn't knock me on the head. Got one of those battery-powered radios in the truck. You all rely on all your fancy technology, but looks like my twenty-dollar radio's the only thing working around here."

Crackling static trailed Abuelo when he returned holding an ancient-looking piece of stone-age tech. A long aluminum antenna projected for three feet.

"Cudjoe Key." A man's exaggerated newscaster voice boomed out from the hundreds of tiny speaker holes. "Ground zero as the storm entered Florida—"

"Confirmed. Keys took the hardest hit." Abuelo's brows furrowed wrangling with the weird antenna wires. "Terrible news for me, but good news for you, Fin, they also announced schools will remain closed all next week."

"How is this good news?" Dad scowled.

"Come on, Victor. Even you were a kid once. All kids like dodging class. Isn't that right?" Abuelo poked me in the ribs.

I grinned from ear to ear. "Very good news!"

"I can take Fin with me to the Keys," Abuelo offered. "Take him off your hands and keep him busy with cleanup. Gonna need an extra set of hands if you can lend him out to me." He shot me a wink.

"Please, Dad, please. Abuelo needs me way more than you. I can help him. Plus, it's not like you trust me to do much anyway," I finished under my breath.

Dad narrowed his eyes. "I do trust you to help me clean up our yard. But after that, you can go with Abuelo for a few days. Only when they give the all-clear that it's safe in the Keys. Got it? And only until school resumes."

"Of course." Abuelo gave me a lopsided smile. "I wouldn't dream of taking him anywhere you deem unsafe."

"Hmph," Dad grunted.

At least I'd get my way.

5
P.U.

Three days later, the announcement blared through Abuelo's antique radio: "US-1 cleared through the Upper Keys. Residents must show ID to get in."

Dad set me free. Yahoo! Because hanging with Abuelo, even if I still had to deal with no Wi-Fi, no hot showers, and no AC, was way better than staying locked home with cranky parents.

Making our way down the Overseas Highway, I imagined an angry giant had also broken free. Using an oversized club, he had stomped his way through the Keys, smashing everything in sight.

Kaboom!

Boats lay tossed on their sides like discarded toys, next to refrigerators and ceramic toilet bowls and endless other objects usually kept *inside* houses. Downed trees and branches were scattered across yards along with rooftops and other things ripped off houses. Some houses were smashed through. Docks had been tossed from the water onto the road. The edges of the street were lined with all kinds of trash for everyone to see.

Ahead of us, a huge GET YOUR KEY LIME PIES HERE sign pointed at a ginormous fallen buttonwood tree. Abuelo swerved to the left, curving around the outer branches at a crawl.

"All these dead trees are depressing." I frowned. "Must be hundreds down."

"Lots of cleanup. Good thing they're only letting islanders back. The true conchs. At least for the next days, it'll keep traffic down."

I pointed out a giant tank. "Is this what it's like driving into war? There're green camouflage trucks all around."

"That one right there's an amphibious vehicle. Moves over land and water like a crocodile. National Guard's been deployed, along with government relief crews. FEMA."

"What does that mean?"

"Federal Emergency Management Agency. They deal

with all this hurricane aftermath. Bring in food and supplies to help people recover."

"How about even having a place to sleep?" I motioned
toward a mattress on the edge of the road.

"Nature's way of purging. Out with the old." Abuelo
sighed. "Irma blew in 'bout sixty miles south. Little past
Seven Mile Bridge but looking mighty close to bull's-eye
around here."

"Good thing it couldn't mess with a train—"

"About to find out if she had her way with my lot."
Abuelo made a sharp right turn into the winding lane
leading down to his house on the bay. When we reached
the end of the road, we both sat and stared in silence
at the jungle that had taken over his home. Palm fronds
and other branches covered the yellow-colored structure, so it looked green instead.

"Still standing." I forced a smile. "Doesn't look like
any trees smashed through your roof."

"No, but they came down everywhere else." His tone
turned drill-sergeant monotone. "Got a machete in
the truck. We'll slash our way through the limbs that
are blocking the driveway." He took a deep breath
before moving the gear shift into park and stepping into
a tangle of branches and leaves.

"Ugh, what's that smell?" I wrinkled my nose, smacking away a mosquito attacking my cheek. More bugs appeared.

"My guess, combo of rotting algae, dead fish, and dirty water. Gonna get real uncomfortable in this heat with no AC. You sure you're up to this?"

"It'll be like camping." My voice faked upbeat while I buried disgust down deep. I steeled myself for battle, flailing my arms and jumping in circles to fight off the swarm of buzzing insects flying in for lunch.

Abuelo didn't waste a minute before jumping into action and swinging the machete around like a powerful sword.

Slash. Crash. Slash. Boom.

Limb after limb fell to the ground, no match for the strength of his strokes.

Meanwhile, I kept myself one rank above useless by carrying the debris to a corner of the yard. An army of biting flies swarmed behind me, playing a game of follow the juicy blood of our leader.

I swatted at the air in a frenzy. "You got any bug spray in the truck?"

"We'll need to get in the house for that. Getting close. Almost cut a clearing. One more branch—" Blade sliced through wood before the machete fell to the ground. Abuelo dropped to his knees, his face bright as the red palm tree berries scattered across the dirt.

"What's wrong?" I ran to his side. "Take a break. I can do the rest."

At least I could try . . .

"I got this," Abuelo grunted. "Just . . . need . . . a minute . . ." He paused. "Hand me one of those waters your mom packed in the cooler."

I tossed him a bottle and braced for one of his long speeches. The usual plastic polluting the oceans. Stewards of the sea—blah, blah, blah—naval pledge and all.

Instead, he closed his eyes, and his breathing became labored again.

"You sure you're okay? Want something to eat? Mami packed my favorite. *Sándwich Cubano.*" My stomach rumbled at the thought of food where I wasn't the main treat.

"I'll pass." Abuelo chugged his water in one gulp and hurled the empty bottle onto a mountain of debris. He crushed the remaining branch with bare hands, squeezed through, and pried open the front door.

I grabbed a sandwich and followed his lead, chomping down on thick slices of ham and pork pressed between crusty bread. Mami had celebrated finding an open *panadería* this morning as though she'd accomplished the greatest feat in the world. Chomping away, I decided she spoke truth.

"Mami also packed your fave, *croquetas*. Don't you wanna take a break and dig in?" I mumbled between bites as the mosquitoes followed me inside and took more nibbles out of me.

"Rest?" Abuelo smirked. "Nonsense. Too much to do." At the back of the house, he ripped open the shutters covering the sliding glass doors leading to the patio deck. "She made it!" He raced down the flight of stairs, closing the distance to the water.

I joined him at the dock and watched him pat *Sirena* with loving strokes.

"My goddess of the sea," he whispered. "No match for your grandma, though." His eyes turned misty. "My real *sirena*. May she rest in peace."

The ocean lapped against the hull of the Whaler with gentle waves—not even a hint it had ever put her in danger. At the end of the canal, where the houses met the bay, it was clear some boats weren't as lucky. A sailboat floated with its keel above the surface, its tall mast plunging into the water and nailing it into a shallow grave.

"Dock took a beating." Abuelo leaned over the sides to inspect the wood. "Gonna have to order some lumber. Get this fixed."

"I can help with hammering and drilling."

"Sure thing. Why I brought you, boy. Let's finish cleaning and see if we can make a trip out soon. Do some scouting."

"Yes, please! Can we go out later today? Please."

"Easy, slick." Abuelo laughed. "Bit soon, but we'll shoot for tomorrow."

"Seriously? I thought it would be days." I broke into a smile, absolutely certain that'd have been the case if Dad had anything to say about it.

"It'll be good to get out and have a look. Storm may have moved things."

"You mean the treasure may have moved?"

Abuelo nodded. "I'll brief you tonight. Still got plenty of daylight to work with. Let's get on with the chopping."

So we did. In addition to him chopping and me carrying, what he didn't mention was there'd be scrubbing and scraping, sloshing through mud, and tons of sweeping. Hours upon hours of cleanup for me to earn my next-level mission briefing. Worth it. A chance to learn more about Abuelo's secrets.

6
ANCIENT HISTORY

As the sun dropped in the sky, Abuelo trekked indoors. I followed him into the hot and humid living space, my body caked in dirt, sweat, and the reek of rotting seaweed I'd cleared from the shoreline.

He walked up to a cabinet with two wooden doors and twisted a tiny black key in the lock. Opening it, he pulled out a stack of maps and journals and balanced them against his chest. After sweeping off an assortment of papers and envelopes cluttering his coffee table, he smacked down the pile.

"I'm about to let you in on all the secrets. The family legacy. But first, we have some gourmet delights to indulge in."

"Yes! I'm starving again." Though the secrets were the real score. And I'd kill for a shower—even cold, but

I swallowed the desire to whine in my throat. I readied up, sitting crisscross on the floor so I didn't ruin his couch.

Abuelo had strolled into the kitchen and grabbed a couple of silver sandwich-sized pouches from a cardboard box stored on the floor of his small pantry. "Dig in," he said as he slapped one in front of me.

I tore open a corner and examined the contents. The food inside resembled dried dog treats better suited for Ratón. "This is dinner?"

"You wanted to go camping." Abuelo grinned. "Been saving these MREs for an emergency. With food and supplies hard to procure, perfect time to put them to use. They only last 'bout ten years."

"Gross. I could eat this when I'm twenty-two?"

"Not as bad as it looks. Gave you a sloppy joe. Not to be confused with Hemingway's old stomping ground, Sloppy Joe's in Key West." Abuelo chuckled and returned to the kitchen, where he grabbed a box of matches.

"Do we cook it at least?"

"Nah. Ready to eat." He struck a match and pulled apart a glass lantern sitting atop the counter before lighting the bottom cylinder. Crafted in brass, it seemed like it belonged on an old ship. One from a long, long time ago before electricity was even invented. "Better than a flashlight. Wouldn't you say?"

We ate in silence for the next few minutes under the warm glow of the flickering flame encased in his ancient light. Once dinner settled like a rock hitting the bottom of my stomach, Abuelo lifted the oldest of the journals and blew off a cloud of dust.

"Let's begin." He caressed the worn leather cover. "This one belonged to my father."

"You mean my great-grandpapa?" I looked him in the eye.

Abuelo nodded.

"Wait," I interrupted. "Before you go on, Dad told me his grandpapa worked on the railroad. The one that fell into the sea. You never told me this part of the story."

Sadness filled Abuelo's eyes. "He did. It's a tragic part of history. Best to let it be."

"But it's my history. Our history. Please don't keep this from me."

Abuelo stayed silent.

"I'm your secret keeper, remember?"

I grinned, showing all my teeth. How could he resist me?

"Very well," Abuelo said. "You do have a right to know about our family."

I did. Especially since Dad hadn't shared any details with me—if he even knew it all.

"My father worked for the rails in Cuba before moving to Key West to join Henry Flagler's crew as a train engineer," he began. "Key West was a main trading port for goods coming in from Havana. Back when the island was free, full of riches. The Pearl of the Caribbean, they called it."

"I can't imagine a free Cuba," I whispered.

"Papá talked about it a lot. He took great pride working for the Overseas Railroad. Its marvel of bridges stretched over the water on the old tracks next to the highway. All the way down to Key West." He pointed south. "Engineering feat of its time. Some called it the eighth wonder of the world."

"Did he"—gulp—"die on the train?"

"He crewed the train that got smashed up during the storm. Engine 447. I'll never forget the number. But no, his guilt was letting others die. You see, the steam locomotive 447 was the only one standing when the tidal wave hit. Papá stood helpless watching passengers trying

51

to escape through shattered windows. Anything to keep from drowning."

"And he hid the treasure?" It was all starting to make more sense.

"No. The treasure belonged to another man. The train was sent from Miami to rescue veterans at a camp in Lower Matecumbe Key, but it never made it past the Islamorada station. Papá left the engine to assist the conductors. It was chaos. He had helped this man board the train at this station. Begged him to leave his baggage behind. It was heavy. A trunk-like metal suitcase. He was slowing down the boarding. People were desperate. Fighting to get on. Not a second to spare. Last chance to get out of the Keys. But turns out it was too late anyway."

"So, what . . . what happened to this man?"

"Refused to part with his luggage. Begged Papá to let him bring it on. Told him it contained treasure. Papá gave in. Regretted it to his last day. He saw the man get washed out with the wave—clinging on to his luggage. Must've been like an anchor sinking him to the bottom of the sea." Abuelo's hand crashed down on the table.

"And it became Great-Grandpapa's quest to search for the gold?"

Abuelo nodded. "He also joined rescue crews to look for people after the hurricane passed. Their deaths haunted him till his last days. His last breath. He died on a deepwater dive, seeking the treasure."

Sadness hung over me like a heavy cloak. "This is so tragic. No wonder you don't like to talk about it."

Abuelo grunted. "Got that right. Let's get back to the books." He flipped through yellow-stained pages. Hand-drawn maps and rows of numbered coordinates were written in black ink.

"What are these?" I pointed at frantic squiggles with arrows and notes.

"Places Papá looked when he began his search eighty-two years ago," Abuelo explained. "He plotted coordinates in grids to cover the miles of ocean floor he scoured. Started from where the train got swept into the ocean."

"This is his handwriting?" I caressed the yellowed page.

"It is. The great Ronaldo Eugenio Santiago Román lives on in these pages."

That's a mouthful. And I complained about my name. "He figured this all out in his head? Without a computer?"

"Ha! Don't think he even owned a TV back then."

"I can't even imagine . . ."

"And this one"—Abuelo picked up another journal—"is mine. It notes where I continued the search after Papá passed. Been trekking farther north, including where we looked the other day. I've marked it here." He indicated a circled area on the larger map underneath the journals. "But I've yet to log it."

"What about that one?" I pointed to a third book. It was smaller than the other two, also bound in leather.

"Also Papá's. We don't need to worry about it for now." He set it aside.

Of course, his answer only made me want to know what it was even more. "Why not?"

"It references other interests Papá had down in Key West. Nothing that will help us." Abuelo stood and walked back to the cabinet.

When he returned, he held a newer notebook in his hand. "This one will be yours. For you to begin tracking your dives. If you want to, that is."

My mouth curved into a big smile. "Yes!" Next-gen treasure hunter. Me. I had big shoes to fill, but I'd never let Abuelo and Great-Grandpapa down.

7
MAYDAY

At dawn, the aroma of fresh coffee tickled my nose. I peeled off the sweaty bedsheets and followed the smell to the kitchen.

"Morning glory." Abuelo held his favorite Navy mug. "Best part of the day, watching the sunrise."

"How'd you even make coffee?"

"Got my old-school *cafetera*." He held up a small aluminum contraption. "And a gas burner. Making coffee, even out in the wild, is an essential part of survival training." He chuckled.

"We still going out today?"

"You betcha. Can't stand the thought of staying cooped up in this oven all day."

He gave me a water from the cooler, and we made a

quick breakfast out of peanut butter and crackers from the pantry.

"What's next on your map? Where we gonna look?"

"Thinking we'll head down by Rodriguez Key. Little northeast of where I've checked."

"So ready to bounce." I clawed at my bare chest. Tiny red swells formed a connect-the-dots running down to my legs.

Abuelo chugged down the last of his coffee. "Them mosquitoes only go after young blood. Don't mess with me anymore."

"Lucky. Should I grab our gear out back?"

"Might as well, but we'll probably only do a recon mission today. See what's out there before we take a plunge. Procure our supplies, sailor, and report to the boat at oh-seven-thirty." Abuelo winked.

"Yes, sir." I saluted and hightailed it to the shed.

As we trolled into the open bay, debris banged against our hull. A thick toxic stench carried through the breeze.

"Ew! Check out the dead fish." I grimaced at the

dozens floating on their sides. "Poor guys already deal with plastic polluting their home, and now this."

"A floating junkyard." Abuelo kept the engine in its lowest gear, dodging piles of trash. Close to shore, overturned boats, trees, wood siding, portions of roofs, banged-up kayaks, and even lawn chairs invaded the sea. "Just terrible." He shook his head and entered the narrow cut between mangroves famously known as Toilet Seat Cut.

"How appropriate. We're entering Potty Lane with all the rest of the trash and it's a miracle—most of the toilet seats are still standing." I pointed at the rows of hand-painted seats lining both sides of the cut. They were staked to the ocean ground on PVC pipes.

"Hail to the throne!" Abuelo said, and snorted.

I knew that the first toilet rim magically appeared here after a hurricane in the early sixties. Washed right onto a post for all the world to see. Locals kept it in place and turned it into a piece of art. Now there were hundreds of them.

"Only darned shame is sandy bottom got all stirred up in the water like it got flushed around in a toilet bowl. Our crystal-clear seas may be gone for a while. It'll be impossible to see."

"It's a crappy bottom messing with our day." Hee-hee. "Get it?" I grinned in spite of my disappointment. "What's the point of even diving?"

"Got that right. No point going down in this murky mess. Unless you got tech." Abuelo grunted.

My mouth dropped open. "Did you just say tech?"

"I'm turning around. Useless to stay out today. Gonna have to get us one of those fancy five-hundred-dollar sonar machines to be able to see what's on the bottom. We'll try again tomorrow."

"You. Technology? Really?"

"You don't think I used all kinds of sophisticated equipment in the Navy? Hell, I trained as an engineer."

"You'd never know," I teased. "We're gonna buy one?"

"Nah, too expensive, plus all the stores are still shuttered. I'm talking loaner. My neighbor, Pete, the captain, uses it to locate his dinner. Sure he won't be doing much fishing for a while."

"Can we borrow it today and go back out? Dad might make me go home soon and we could miss our chance."

Abuelo crinkled his forehead, and I braced myself for the "No" Dad would have given me for sure. Instead, his wrinkles gave way to a smile. "Good point. Why waste today? *Carpe diem.* Let's swing by Captain Pete's place."

"Yes! Carpe whatever . . . You're the coolest abuelo ever."

"Truth be to that." He grinned. "*Carpe diem* is Latin for 'Seize the day.' Live for the present. Today!"

"I like it." I shot a fist in the air. "It can be our treasure hunting motto."

"Let's add another one to the mix: *Semper fortis*. It's the Navy's motto, which means, 'Always strong.'"

"Good one. *Semper fortis*," I repeated. I would do my best to be mighty. "Like . . . you," I said.

He shot me a thumbs-up.

At Pete's dock, Abuelo jumped out and was back in five minutes with the equipment. As he wired it in on the console and jumped in the shallow water to attach the transducer on the stern, he explained how the fish finder worked by sending out sound waves and creating a picture based on how long it took for the sound waves to bounce off whatever was underneath the boat and come back to the machine. Turning it on at the dock, we could see the ghostly shape of the ocean floor just underneath us. It even showed us shapes that Abuelo said were fish. New old tech at the ready, we headed to Rodriguez Key the same afternoon.

When we got to the spot that Abuelo wanted to search, we trolled very slowly back and forth. The picture on the screen wasn't always clear. "How will we ever find a trunk with this?" I complained. "It was hard enough when we were diving."

"Never told you this would be a simple mission. We can give up, or we can have fun trying, and enjoy fresh mosquito-free breeze."

He cut off the engine and for a while we just drifted on the smooth ocean surface, the gentle waves lapping against the boat.

"Have fun, for sure." I glanced at the collection of red swells decorating my body. "But this is way harder than finding pirate treasure. It would be easier if your map had a big X-marks-the-spot, and we could take a shovel and dig it up on some secret key."

Abuelo held his chest, breaking into a throaty laugh. Laughter that led to coughing. Lots of coughing. "Sun's getting to your brain, Fin. I already told you this isn't a bedtime story. That would be way too easy. The hunt's half the fun, wouldn't you say?"

"But seriously, there're lots of sandbars and small keys

around. You think it could have washed up on the sand somewhere?"

"Anything's po—possible," Abuelo choked out between coughs.

I patted his back. "You okay? You look pale."

Abuelo turned the ignition key. "Gotta . . . head back . . ." His voice came out low and slurred as the engine growled to life. He stumbled back against the captain's chair, gripping his chest before his eyes rolled back, exposing the white parts in all the wrong ways.

"What's wrong?" I asked, and he didn't answer. I had to control the panic kicking in with the big thumps pounding inside me. I grabbed hold of his shoulders, trying to steady him. Help him breathe. Anything.

Abuelo bumped a fist to his chest and shook his index finger at the steering wheel. He opened his mouth to speak.

Nothing came out.

The right side of his face drooped, and his sun-wrinkled skin sagged before his head twisted to the side at an awkward angle. His last move as he sank back in the captain's chair.

My heartbeat raced up to a wild rhythm. I opened my mouth to cry. To scream.

I remained as muted as him. Besides, we were in the middle of the ocean. What would be the use?

"Abuelo! Abuelo!" I shook him gently.

No response.

I had to do something. Quick.

I pulled out a towel from my duffel, rolled it up, and placed it around his neck to prop up his head. My fingers shook, feeling around his neck. In movies, this seemed the way to determine if an injured person was . . . alive.

I sucked in my breath.

Please, God. Please let there be a pulse.

I finally found the right spot. A faint beat responded to my touch. Then I saw his chest rising and falling as he took quick, shallow breaths.

Relief washed over me. *Alive. Not dead.*

I fought for control, pushing away the darker thoughts invading my mind: *Not dead. Yet . . .*

I had to keep Abuelo alive. I was the only chance he'd get.

If only I could remember all the complicated medical stuff I crammed last year in life science class. Heimlich? CPR? Why didn't I pay more attention?

I said a silent prayer in my mind:

Please, God, please.
Help me remember.
Keep Abuelo alive.
If you do, I promise to do better, be better.
I'll even pray to Mami's santos.
Especially the Virgin of Charity, who helped another
boy at sea.
Please. Please. Please.

I had to concentrate. Dig deep in my brain where all the school stuff got sorted and erased.

Dummies. It's all that popped in my head. We had practiced reviving dummies. Though now I was the useless dummy.

They were creepy and plastic. Plastic and . . . dead.

No. No. No. Abuelo's not dead. I couldn't let him be dead.

Hysteria danced inside my head. Not. Dead. Yet. Not. Dead. Yet.

I bit on my chapped lips until a metallic taste prickled against my tongue.

Blood. Band-Aid. First aid.

Yes. Yes. This was it! The first-aid kit. Abuelo kept one on board.

I bent down, snatched the plastic box from a water-proof drawer under the steering wheel, and yanked the white lid open.

Bandages, steri-strips, and aspirin tumbled out. Dumb idea.

Dummy. Dummy. Dummy.

How could any of this stuff even help? I couldn't shove a pill down his mouth and make him all better.

Not. Dead. Yet.

Panic pulsed like a wave electrifying every inch of my body. I had to find something useful. Anything.

Bonk.

My head banged against the metal steering wheel in the narrow space. The radio receiver crashed down when my hand shot up to massage what Mami would call a *chichón*—right before she'd launch into chanting her cringey *sana, sana, culito de rana* Puerto Rican cure-all. As if her rhyme about healing a little frog's butt could ever help.

Just then the solution smacked me right where the giant lump of hurt was forming.

The radio!

It's what Abuelo was pointing toward. Not the wheel.

He wanted me to call for help. And if he knew he needed help, then this was a really big deal.

I cradled the receiver in my left hand. My other hand trembled, turning a small knob to the right. Bringing the radio to life.

Next challenge: locate emergency channel.

Sixteen. I knew this much.

Oh, and figure out how to work this thing. Details . . .

Seemed easy enough in the movies, but in real life, not so much.

I pressed down on the transmit button. A small drop of hope fluttered in the pit of my stomach. "Mayday. Mayday. Mayday. Calling from the *Sirena*. Mayday."

Crackling static answered my call.

"Mayday. Mayday. Mayday," I repeated. "I need help. Please!"

More static.

"Mayday. Anyone there? Help me."

Static.

"Mayday. PLEASE! PLEASE!"

I banged the receiver back into place.

A man's voice erupted from the speaker. "This is the

U.S. Coast Guard responding. What's your emergency? Over."

YES! I shot a fist in the air and, as Mami would do, made the sign of the cross. I owed her *santos* and the charity lady a special prayer.

"My grandfather passed out. I think he had a heart attack. Over."

"Son, is there another adult with you? Over."

"No, only my grandfather. Over."

"How old are you? Over."

Shoot. "Um." Why'd he have to ask? I struggled with exaggerating a bit, adding a few years to my age, but no, he'd eventually find out. "Twelve years old. Over."

"Do you know your coordinates? Your location? We'll send out a rescue team. Over."

"I can drive to save time. I have my boater's license. My grandfather needs help. He will . . . die. Over."

A long pause followed. My stomach tied up in knots. Waiting. This is where the official officer guy would tell me I was only a kid and couldn't be counted on to help in the rescue. But I could. I knew it. I'd do anything. It was my abuelo. "Hello. Hello. I can drive. Over."

Coast Guard man's voice boomed to life again. "I need your coordinates. Over."

"Near Rodriguez Key. Over. But again, I can pilot the boat!"

"Can you navigate to Trunk Cay Marina? Do you know where it is? Over."

Phew. "Yes!" He believed in me. "I mean, roger that. I mean, on my way. Over." The receiver dropped to the floor, hanging on its coiled cord.

He gave me a chance. This was it. I wouldn't let the U.S. Coast Guard down. I wouldn't let Abuelo down.

I had the most important mission of my life to execute. I had trained for this. Abuelo had trained me. I could drive the boat. This time on my own.

But first, I had to secure Abuelo. Make sure he didn't slip when I switched to high speed. I grabbed a line and secured him to one side of the captain's seat. After that, I wedged my body tightly next to him and took the wheel.

Left hand firm at the helm, I yanked the gear shift into full throttle, pushing back the strands of summer-long hair covering my eyes. Nothing could get in my way. I had to save Abuelo.

The boat sliced over gray-blue ocean, cutting through whitecapped waves. Water sprayed over the windshield. Some droplets missed the plastic and felt like invisible pellets spattering against my face, hitting with the same intensity as the thoughts pounding in my brain. I can't lose Abuelo . . . Can't. Won't.

The sea mixed in with the salty tears already clouding my eyes. I fought to keep them peeled over the horizon. Fought to keep going. Full force. Pushing on and on in a trance-like state. Chanting: steady to port, steady to shore.

Narrow angling cuts through desolate mangrove fields displayed a tangle of roots. They anchored them to the shallow water, making it difficult to steer. On and on they guarded the shoreline—miles and miles of emptiness. I raced past blurs of red and green channel markers, doing my best to stay in the tight space between them. Keep from running aground in the low tide of late afternoon.

Usually the water would be dotted with late-day fishermen, casting their lines, trying their luck for a bite. But nobody was out today. Recovering from the storm was the only thing on everyone's mind. I was completely alone.

I glanced at Abuelo's unconscious body and rubbed the shark-tooth necklace he gave me. It hung around my neck on a leather cord—every day since my tenth birthday. If only it could pass on his strength. Make me feel less alone.

But no, a torment of thoughts drowned me.

I could hear my father as I raced to save his father: Why didn't we make the safe choice and stay home?

8
METAL BIRD

A pelican rested on a wooden stake jutting out of the water. Right behind his brown feathered body, a big red circle popped into view with the words: IDLE SPEED NO WAKE spelled out. This was code for an ocean kind of stop sign. Sort of a yellow traffic light meaning go at a crawl. Slow.

I shifted to lowest gear—the opposite of where my pulse was taking me to make the final trek in. One last turn and the marina appeared in front. Empty except for a Coast Guard boat tied to the dock.

Two figures in blue uniforms and caps stood at the edge of the dock. The taller one with a beard yelled as I approached. "Easy, son. Cut your engine and throw me your line."

I let out the breath I'd been holding and fought back

the tears burning my eyes. Abuelo's rescue team. I'd have help to save him. At last.

"I'm Officer Bernard." The man grabbed the rope I threw him from the bow. "You holding up okay?" He studied my face. "Bit of a haul for you down south, but it's where I could get—" He craned his neck up and pointed.

A loud buzzing sound swallowed up any answer I could give. Good thing. Because no, how could I possibly be okay with any of this? My *semper fortis* was running on empty.

The noise got louder and louder until I could feel the vibration, tingling my skin with its electric charge. A jolt. A dose of reality kicking my butt. This was all going down at high speed. For real.

A large metal bird dropped from the sky. The red-and-white Coast Guard medevac helicopter settled on an open patch of grass. Palm trees, already battered by the hurricane, bordered the field, fronds thrashing in the wind from the rotor.

Officer Bernard and the other coastguard boarded the boat. While his partner untied the rope and tended to Abuelo, Officer Bernard waved toward the whirlwind of activity surrounding the helicopter. Two men had popped out wheeling a stretcher.

"They'll take good care of your grandfather."

"Can they . . . they . . . they save him?" Could be my only hope.

"Son, they'll do all they can." His tone became gentle. "Disembark your vessel. Let's give the team space to do their job." He led me off the boat and out of the way as the medics raced down the dock. "Either of your parents around? Have you called them?"

"No, my phone's dead. Couldn't charge it without electricity. And my mom and dad live in Miami."

"Perfect." Officer Bernard pulled out his cell. "Number?"

Perfect? How is any of this perfect? I wanted to scream.

"I'll have them meet you at Baptist Hospital in Miami. Your grandfather will be transported to the mainland as a precaution. His condition may need more intense treatment than what he can receive with the hurricane crippling operations down here."

Panic coursed through my veins. "His condition? What is it?"

Officer Bernard stayed quiet.

"Will he . . . will he be all right?"

"I can't say. But I do know our paramedics and the doctors at the hospital will do everything they can.

Follow me, please." He prodded me along. "You'll go with him and leave the boat here."

"Will it be safe? It's his *Sirena*. My duty is to take care of her. He'd expect me to. If anything happened to her . . . I'd . . . disappoint him."

"Yes. Yes. We'll arrange it with the marina. But come back with your folks to retrieve her, you hear? You're too young to be navigating without an adult, though you handled yourself well. You did indeed."

"Thank you." My chest swelled for a second before the air whizzed out. Replaced with guilt. Regret. I should have never egged Abuelo to go out today.

We stopped short. "This is where I leave you."

Up close and personal, the helicopter seemed way bigger than the news one I'd waved to in the air only days earlier as Abuelo drove.

Too much had changed in less than a week.

I stared at the thick blades protruding high above its roof. "I'm . . . I'm going in that?" A flicker of excitement mixed in with the fear already rumbling inside my stomach.

"Does it pose a problem, young man?"

"No. No. Not at all." *Semper fortis. Semper fortis.* I dug deep. "I mean, I've always wanted to ride in one. They're cool and all. I just didn't think it would be . . . like, an emergency."

"You got this." Officer Bernard helped me into the cabin. "Keep the faith, kid." He stepped back, making way for the medics to lift the stretcher.

Once I was inside the surprisingly large cabin, the pilot turned back and greeted me with a curt salute. Blond hair pressed against her face, peeking out from a headset. "First time on one of these birds?" Her gaze softened when she connected with my stare.

I nodded.

"It'll be a piece of cake for you. Strap into the jump seat." She pointed. "Give my partners room to work so they can get your grandpa stabilized."

I clicked the thick belt over my chest at the same time they snapped two giant red seat belts holding Abuelo in place. The medics got busy. They dabbed, prodded, and poked. Stuck big, scary needles and tubes into Abuelo's lifeless-looking body, covered his mouth and nose with an oxygen mask, and added stickers to his chest, connecting spaghetti-like cords into monitors. Life-saving machines, I hoped.

Beep, beep, beep became the constant noise till the blades took over. They whirred back to life, overpowering all other sounds in a deafening roar. I shrunk in my seat, hands over ears.

"That will help," said one of the medics. She pointed to a headset hanging next to my seat. I put it on, cutting down the noise to a more tolerable roar.

Swoosh.

Off we went. Straight up in the air, my pulse rising quickly as we climbed. Below, Officer Bernard waved bye-bye. He became smaller and smaller the higher we rose in the sky.

I closed my eyes, a mix of emotions blending inside me—half excitement, half fear. Would we drop from the air?

No. Guilt flooded over me for any enjoyment I felt as the helicopter leaned to the left and lurched forward in a movement that pressed me back into my seat. A wave of fresh tears moistened my eyes, taking over the moment of thrill I got from enjoying the ascent. Fun wasn't the point of this life-or-death mission. I couldn't lose Abuelo.

I stared out the window and toyed with the shark-tooth necklace. The perkiness of the day—bright blue skies and puffy clouds—clashed against my mood. The world down below looked peaceful and perfect. Even the skinny stretch of the Overseas Highway was mesmerizing as it wound its way over land and water that was sparkling bright as an emerald. Way too beautiful for this ugly situation.

Staring down, I imagined the original railroad chugging along when tracks covered this roadway. These weren't happy thoughts. It was all because of the train. The treasure. It almost got Abuelo killed. Great-Grandpapa had died searching for it. It could be cursed!

Bridges connected the narrow landmasses rising from the sea. Tavernier popped into view, followed by Key Largo. This longest key Abuelo called home. In Spanish, *largo* means long. Looking down from the sky, I could see it extending for miles and miles. The name made sense.

The tallest bridge of all marked the exit from the chain of islands. It was from this spot, only days ago, I had seen a waterspout. Abuelo had sat next to me. Strong. In charge. So different in a matter of days. He lay helpless now, and I had to be the one taking charge.

The view turned imperfect to match my brooding when we crossed the Everglades. Never-ending swampy patches of mangroves and sawgrass took over the land-scape. Dead, dried-out trees, toppled by the hurricane, added splotches of brown to the green. Lots of brown.

I could deal with seeing brown.

The 'glades turned to farmland and then a thickening pattern of roads, houses, neighborhoods. Swimming pools, golf courses, parking lots, malls. Soon it became a tight grid of city streets. We descended as a large peach-colored building came into view. When it was underneath us, the chopper leaned right and hovered above a large red square on the roof painted with a large white cross with an *H* at its center, which announced we'd arrived at the place that could help Abuelo.

We dropped down. Straight down. A giant balloon being plucked from the sky. We touched down on the hospital helipad with a soft thud that seemed to set off invisible get-up-and-go alarms. The medical team sprang to life, undoing belts, detaching monitors, and untangling tubes and cords. I stayed buckled in. Praying. Wishing the world would stop spinning out of control.

Only the blades responded. The spinning stopped. Though not the buzzing. The vibration kept going. On and on it circled inside my head like a tormenting bee.

Seeding fear that at any moment, Abuelo's life could buzz away from me.

With a clank and a snap, the door opened from the outside. A man and a woman appeared wearing light-blue scrubs. They yanked Abuelo's body out, wheeling him away in his metal bed. Away from me . . .

"Wait!" I undid my belt and scrambled out to chase after them. "I'm part of his rescue team."

"Come with me, sweetie." A female nurse appeared out of nowhere, grabbing hold of my arm. "I'll take you to the waiting room. You can't follow him to the ER. We need to let the doctors do their job."

My hands balled into fists. "I don't want to leave my grandpa."

"I know you don't." The nurse patted my shoulder, softening her grip. "Are your parents here?"

"I called them. Actually, the Coast Guard officer did."

"Good. Good." She continued to pat me down like a stray puppy, leading me down a long hall on her invisible leash.

I followed blindly.

"Are you hungry? I can find you something to eat. How about some ice cream?" she asked in a sugary voice. "Sound good?"

"Thank you." I tried not to be rude. But seriously, ice cream? At a time like this? Did she think I was a two-year-old?

"Here we are." The nurse opened the door to a room full of chairs and sofas. Ice-cold air greeted me along with the sound of my name. My full name.

Mami rushed to my side. "Fernando Javier Cordero Román. *Mi amor.* My big boy." She embraced me into a cloud of her violet perfume. "Are you okay?"

I slumped into her arms, feeling small as can be. Tears ran free. "No. Abuelo's bad. They took him away from me."

Dad had stood up when I came into the room, but he hadn't moved. When I pulled away from Mami and looked at him, instead of a "hello," he shot me one of his you-disappointed-me-again looks. I knew what was coming before he started speaking.

"What were you thinking, son? I let you go with your grandfather to help. Not to have him take you on a joy-ride after the hurricane. You two had no business putting your lives in danger."

I stared at the linoleum tiles. Anything to avoid his brown-eyed daggers. Because he was right. This was all my fault, and I was the worst grandson in the whole wide world. I couldn't save Abuelo. His father. I should have never begged him to take me out.

"*Tranquilo.* Can't you see Fernando is already crying? You're making him feel worse." Mami shook a long red fingernail at Dad as if it were a magic wand able to shove all the hurtful words back through his lips.

Not possible.

Dad's expression closed up while Mami continued to encourage him to chillax from the sidelines in her usual way. "*Paciencia.* Give Fernando a break. Let him explain."

But no. It wasn't going to work this time. Dad wasn't buying it and I didn't deserve it. I sat down and slumped back in a chair. Easier to stare at the floor: *Swallow me.*

I couldn't explain away guilt. What would be the use?

Now we all sat in silence. The occasional ticking of the round wall clock remained the only sound in the room.

Five, ten, fifteen, twenty minutes passed before the nurse burst back in, slicing through the tension.

"Ice cream makes everything better," she said in singsong, plastering on a big smile before handing me a small container and plastic spoon.

Dad stood and approached her. Bitterness still rang in

his tone. "Miss, you've left us waiting for half an hour. Is there news about my father's condition? I only got attention when I had his insurance forms to fill."

The nurse stiffened, the curl of her lips turning upside down. "The doctor will be out to brief you as soon as possible." She turned on her heels and pressed an ID badge onto a panel, opening big double doors.

"Wait." Dad sped after her.

"I'm sorry, sir." Her manner remained abrupt. "There's no other news." The off-limit barricades closed behind her.

Dad clenched his hands before retreating to his seat, opposite of me. "Hours to wait," he grumbled. "And nothing else—"

"Except this." I slammed the ice cream into a trash can.

Only Mami remained calm. "The energy you put out in the world is what you get back." She stared at Dad before pressing a rosary between her palms. Her eyelids closed and her lips moved in silence.

She must've mustered all the powers that be, calling upon some small miracle. When she opened her eyes, Dad moved to sit next to me. Repentance played across his face. "Sorry for losing my cool, son. Go on. Tell me everything."

I chewed on my bottom lip before all the emotion burst out of me. "I . . . I . . . I tried to save him," I cried. "I did my best."

"I've been harsh." He pulled me into a hug. "I'm sure you did everything you could. Dad had a lot of stress with the hurricane. He's a tough old man, but he's not invincible. This was all too much for him. Too, too much." He shook his head.

It became harder to breathe. *Invincible*. Yes. That's how I always thought of Abuelo. He would fight. He had to. Same way he fought all his life to find treasure. I would help him this time. Save him. It was up to me.

I began to formulate a plan in my mind.

9
BIG ENOUGH

After several hours of making sure the waiting room lived up to its name, the doctor finally appeared. Using all sorts of big, fancy words, he explained Abuelo had had a hemorrhagic stroke—his super complicated way of saying a blood vessel in his head had broken and allowed blood to leak out and put pressure on part of his brain. Emergency surgery had been needed to relieve the pressure and repair the blood vessel. He also told us it could take months for him to recover. For his brain to work like normal again.

It hit me like a blow in the gut. But at least we didn't get worse news. Abuelo had survived, and the next day we'd get to see him. Maybe he would even be awake.

Early the next morning, we were back at the hospital. As we walked into the intensive care unit, the sharp smell of sterilizing chemicals (think diving into a bottle of rubbing alcohol) attacked my nose. When we entered his room, Abuelo lay asleep in his bed, looking an ashen color in place of his normally suntanned face. A band of gauze was wrapped around his head, holding a large pad in place. Grunt-snores escaped from his mouth instead of his normally booming voice. Yet, at that moment, the snores were the very best sound in the world. Snoring equaled life.

Dad cleared his throat, spurring the loudest grunt-snore of all.

Abuelo fought to pry open his eyes. Two-ton weights and a thick coat of sleep gook seemed to shut them in place. He managed a peek through tiny slits and opened his mouth.

CROAK.

It's all that came out. A strange frog sound along with drops of drool sliding down his chin. Dad had nailed it yesterday. Abuelo looked the opposite of invincible. And it was my fault. I'd stuck him in bed.

A nurse, different one today, walked in wearing a painted-on grin to match the smiley-face-emoji print of her scrub top.

"Good morning! I'm Isabel," she said, and waved a gloved hand. She turned to examine Abuelo. "Super! You're awake. Making excellent progress, Mr. Román."

I leaped to the opposite side of his bed. "If he's so great, why can't he speak?" What I really wanted to do was wipe away all the annoying little smiles on her shirt and face.

She shook her head with a sad little nod, for once losing her perma-grin. "These things take time. He'll find his voice."

Abuelo's hands jerked around in an awkward motion to fight off the feeding tubes and cords tying him in place. Frustration and pain registered in his eyes. They darted across the room.

"No, no, no, Mr. Román, you can't be ripping things off." Smiley nurse shook her finger at Abuelo. She reached under the bed and retrieved a plastic, oval-shaped bucket. "Bedpan? For ur-i-na-tion?" she whispered.

"He pees in that thing?" I asked in shock.

"Let's say urinate," Dad chided.

"His personal porta-potty," the nurse said, as if it was no big deal. "If you can step outside for about fifteen minutes—give him a little privacy—I'll clean him up with a sponge bath and check his vitals. Get him ready for a proper visit."

Abuelo's hands continued to flail. I bet it was his only way to complain about having a female nurse attend to all his private needs. Uff, he'd be freaking for days.

The nurse shooed us out. "You'll be more comfortable if you go to the waiting room. I'll come get you when he's ready."

Walking down the corridor, the plan I'd started thinking about yesterday crystallized in my head. A mission to finish what Abuelo started. A way to make him better. Make him proud of me.

I cornered Dad the second he sat. "We need to drive down and pick up Abuelo's boat from the marina."

He frowned. "You told me what happened, but why the rush? They are still trying to get back on their feet down there in the Keys. It doesn't make any more sense now than it did two days ago."

Here we go . . . Beatdown from Dad. Round two.

I shrugged, picking at the calluses on my hand from all of my clean-up work. Hard to believe that was only two days ago.

"Be honest." His tone softened. "I'm trying to understand."

I wriggled in the plastic seat for a solid five minutes. The truth was, I'd need his help now that Abuelo was tied to a bed. But which version of the real truth could I share with him?

"Go on, or I may lose patience," Dad prodded.

"Easy, *dale*. Fernando, tell us what's going on," Mami encouraged me.

"It's just . . . it's just . . . it's a family secret. Abuelo swore me to secrecy."

He chose only me . . .

"We're not your family?" The hurt in Mami's voice rang clear. "We would do anything for you. And for Abuelo. Families stick together."

She had me at "Abuelo." Plus, it's not like I had much choice. I sucked in my breath. Here goes . . .

"Would you believe me if I said we were hunting for treasure?"

There. The secret was out. It now hung over us like a heavy weight. But at least I had unleashed the crushing burden from myself.

The only other person occupying the room, an old lady sitting in a corner holding two giant needles and a ball of yarn to match her gray hair and dress, looked up.

"Whoa! Treasure?" Dad only just stopped short of a yell. "What in the world are you talking about?"

The old lady placed her supplies on her lap and stared, ready to enjoy the show.

I drew a finger to my mouth, signaling in her direction. Abuelo did warn about greedy pirates trying to take our loot. Though even I had to chuckle at the mental image of this sweet grandmother-type doing anything evil.

"Go on," Dad whispered, plucking me from my daydream right when the old lady raised her pointy needle swords and went back to her knitting.

"It fell off the train during that 1930s hurricane. Into the sea," I whispered. "Abuelo's father told him the story. He was there."

"You mean my abuelo? You mentioned the train stuff before, but now you claim there's treasure?"

"It's all real. No one else knows. It's my turn to find it."

Dad's face turned a bright shade of red. "This was my dad's latest harebrained scheme?"

Mami gasped. "Victor, por favor. He's lying on a hospital bed. Listen to what Fernando has to say. Patiently."

I thanked Mami with my eyes. Then, in whispers, I told them about the notebooks, about the man with the suitcase, both lost in the storm. About Abuelo's search, and my great-grandpapa's search.

Dad rolled his eyes but stayed silent. I carried on, keeping an eye on gray yarn lady, who seemed to be leaning in to listen. I lowered my voice still further. "I couldn't sleep last night since I was worried about

Abuelo, and I googled a bunch of maps. Did a ton of research. Jotted down ideas on where we can look."

"Wait a minute." Dad put a hand out. "We? You can't possibly think I'm going to play along with this crazy scheme?" Annoyance colored his face again. "Especially at a time like this. If it even exists . . ."

Mami shot Dad a piercing look. "Victor, you asked him to be honest with you."

Dad threw his hands up in the air. "But I didn't expect—"

"Never mind." I pushed off my chair. "I should have known better than to trust you. I'll do it on my own. I'll find it for him. It'll make him all better."

"Now you've really lost your marbles if you think some fantasy of yours is going to cure him. He's an old man. He's had a stroke. He needs science. Medicine."

"Victor!" Mami scolded again.

"Enough of this nonsense! I don't want to hear any more of this crazy talk. You got that?"

I crossed my arms, forming a shield over my chest. "Got it. I knew you wouldn't understand. You're nothing like Abuelo. No wonder he didn't bother sharing the family secret with you."

Dad was a kettle about to blow. Even gray lady shrunk back into her corner of the room.

I'd pushed too far.

Long silent minutes ticked off on the clock hanging over my head.

Tick. Tick. Tock.

I couldn't take it anymore. "Are you going to say something? Anything?"

Anger melted to a guilty look, sweeping across Dad's face. "You're right. I don't think I will ever understand, but at least I will listen."

My mouth dropped open. That'd be a first . . . But no chance he could ever get me.

"Let me start with this. I'm proud of how you handled yourself, Fernando. Calling the Coast Guard and getting the boat back to shore. You showed self-reliance."

I blew out my chest because, WOW! That sure did sound like a compliment.

"You think you can also start listening to me when I ask you to call me Fin? Like Abuelo," I couldn't resist throwing in. "Everyone calls me Fin. Fernando is too formal. Doesn't even sound like me."

"Fin." Dad let the name roll off his tongue as though

he were being introduced to a foreign language. "It'll take some getting used to."

Mami smiled. "To me you're always *mi amor*."

"Unless you're mad at me," I said with a chuckle. "Then I get the quadruple-name punch."

Dad looked sheepish. "I'll try to be more supportive."

Hope bubbled inside. This was my opening. Maybe the only chance I'd get. "I know the perfect way."

"Go on."

Gotcha! I hid a grin. "After we pick up Abuelo's boat, I . . . I need you to be my dive buddy. To find the treasure!"

Dad stood up with a jerk, scraping his chair against the polished floor. He paced back and forth, running his fingers through his hair. "Dive buddy? I haven't even agreed to help you hunt for it."

"But who else can I—"

"Besides, I don't dive. Don't know how to. Don't even know how to drive a boat."

"Relax." I tried to sound grown up. "I won't make you actually dive, or even drive the boat. I only need someone to go out with me. I can make the dives on my own. You can snorkel."

Dad shook his head. "Snorkel? Don't do that either. You

know I don't even like going into the ocean. Too many slimy creatures to worry about. And sharks. Barracudas. No. No. No. I'm sorry. You're asking too much. No can do."

"Then you'll wait on the boat. I'll wrap a rope around me and tug if I get into trouble. I saw a guy do it in a movie once. It worked."

"This is real life. And that all sounds dangerous. What could I even do if there was a problem? And who's going to drive the boat?"

Duh! "Me."

"You?"

"I have my boating license, but since I'm underage, I can't go out without an adult present. That would be you." I shot him double-handed pointers. "You don't need to do anything. I'll handle everything."

Mami stared in awe. "You can drive?"

"Yeah, what do you mean you have your boating license?" Dad cut in. "How is that even possible? You're only eleven."

"Twelve," I corrected. "Just turned twelve."

"*¿Te olvidaste?*" Mami accused. "We celebrated his birthday during the hurricane."

"Temporary memory lapse." A shadow of guilt flitted across Dad's face.

"Abuelo taught me all the boat handling stuff, and for the license part, I did an online course—all by myself. Last summer. I passed the test on the first try, and I have an official license." A boating safety education card, to be exact, I left out, but it was legit. "I can show you. I'm a good captain. Abuelo lets me drive all the time."

"He does, huh?" Dad snorted. "You never told me all this."

"You never cared about the things I did with Abuelo."

"I'm sorry if I didn't seem interested." He met my eyes. "It's not that I don't care. I've never understood all the things you two like. Never shared your sense of adventure. Dad's made a point of reminding me of this my whole life."

"It's okay. Abuelo and I have a saying: *carpe diem*. It means seize the day, live for the present. It's not too late to have an adventure. Do it for Abuelo."

"I'll . . . I'll try." Dad's face showed dread, as though I were asking him to commit a crime.

Me, I allowed a hopeful smile. Because SCORE! I was back on track!

Not long after this, Abuelo's nurse appeared in the doorway and told us he was ready for a visit. This time, her smiley-face scrubs didn't annoy me at all.

10
SLIPPETY SLY

Dad agreed to drive down with me and fetch the boat. Two days later at sunrise, I buckled in before Dad could get on my case and we pulled out of our driveway. Mami waved us off from the front door. Morning rays illuminated her face, shining a spotlight on the plastic tarp hanging above her. Our roof was covered in blue instead of the usual brick red.

Dad hit the brakes. "Almost forgot." He pushed the gear back into park, then programmed a driving app and plugged in his phone. "Phew. Only way to charge around here."

"And only way to get AC." I cranked up the air to the highest setting. Even a week post-Irma, electricity wasn't happening in our neighborhood. "Don't you know the way to Abuelo's by heart?"

"Some roads are still closed with fallen wires or debris. This'll reroute us," he said, getting the car underway again.

I leaned back, eyes closed, hiding a smirk. I'd do my best to get along, but I couldn't help thinking Abuelo wouldn't have missed this opening to poke fun at Dad. I'd give anything to hear the two of them bickering again. "Poking the bear," he called it. Not like Dad had any wild in him, of course, though I could try to stoke it out of him.

What seemed like minutes later, the car jolted to a stop again. My eyes popped open. We were in front of Abuelo's house.

"We've arrived," Dad announced. "Sleep well? You snored louder than your grandfather." He grabbed his cell again. "Safe to text now. What's the name of the marina we're heading to?"

"Trunk Cay. In Islamorada." I yawned, stretching my arms.

He adjusted his glasses over his nose before pecking away at his phone. The irony of the name toyed with me. Trunk. We were looking for a treasure trunk. Could be one of those omen thingies—but who knew if it was good or evil. So far, all I'd had was bad luck.

"Go in and grab whatever gear you need. It'll be dark in there. Take this." Dad handed me a small flashlight. "Making a quick run to the pharmacy we passed. Seems the only thing open out here yet. Hurricane wreckage just kept getting worse heading south." Dad shook his head.

A half hour passed before he returned, and I climbed back into the family sedan.

"Ready?" Dad looked up from the wheel. Pink lips and dark eyes peered under a canopy of straw. All that was visible through the globs of white sunscreen streaked over his face and over every exposed part of his skin. He'd switched out a polo shirt for pharmacy-chic island attire: a tacky flowered shirt.

"Ahh! What'd you do to yourself? No wonder you took so long. You're only missing the tourist stamp on your forehead." I should've held back the jab. Too hard to resist.

"Ha, ha," Dad snorted. "Picked up sunblock along with this hat and shirt. But the real coup de grâce was snagging a first-aid kit." He reached onto the back seat and grabbed a large plastic box.

"There's already a small one on the boat." Not a good memory. "You don't need to bring this ginormous thing and take up room for your coup de whatever."

"I'm sure this one is more complete." He grinned, baring his front teeth like a beaver would, so they shone bright as his face.

"And ridiculously big . . ."

"We're doing things my way—with caution. And speaking of, you gotta put sunscreen on. You'll risk skin cancer if you don't."

"I think you got enough on for both of us. Besides, it's not even sunny."

"Not negotiable." He handed me a bottle. "Put down your visor and make sure you cover every inch of your skin."

Groan. I bit my tongue and followed his orders. A good little boy.

After a short drive north, we arrived at the marina. The second I stepped out of the car, a stranger approached.

"Victor Roman?" the man asked Dad. He pronounced our last name without emphasizing the last syllable. Mami would have had a fit if she were here. "Accent on the *a*," she annoyingly corrected people.

The man extended a tattooed arm. "Sly Jerome here. At your service."

Dad returned the handshake. "A pleasure. This is my son, Fernando." He waved in my direction.

"Fin," I said, correcting Dad for the hundredth time.

"Gotcha." Sly gave me a lopsided smile without bothering to extend his hand again.

Who was this creep?

I stood tall, puffing out my chest while his beady eyes peered over mirrored lenses to examine me head to toe. Darned if I'd let him think I was built like a wimpy sixth grader. After all, I had been saving up my *semper fortis* these last few days. Or at least I'd fake it.

"We'll grab our stuff and meet you by the boat, Sly. Where exactly is it?" Dad asked me.

I stayed silent. The reason for Sly's appearance was getting way too obvious.

"Fin. Tell him, please."

"End of the dock," I grunted. "*Sirena*. The Whaler."

"I'll start loading tanks." Sly slinked away.

"Who. Is. He?" I asked. At this point, it was a stupid question.

"I hired him to escort you on your dives. He's a certified instructor and will accompany us on this boondoggle of yours. I checked the regulations. Divers your age need to go under with a certified adult. And you can't pilot a boat on your own until you're fourteen. Wasn't easy finding someone to go out so soon after the hurricane."

My mouth dropped open in a wide O. "Are you kidding me? I don't need a babysitter. It was supposed to be you and me. For once . . ."

Dad folded his arms across his chest. "I've made up my mind. It's the only way I'll go."

"He'll find out about our treasure." I had to knock some sense into Dad, get through his thick *coco* of a skull—what Mami would call it when she got annoyed. "Abuelo said it's a family secret. How could you let anyone in on this?"

"I didn't give anything away. His only job is to make sure you're safe. I don't know the first thing about diving or boating. If we're going to do this, it's safety first."

I rolled my eyes. "Safety first," I mimicked under my

breath. "It's just like you to ruin this. Of course, he'll figure out what we're looking for. And, like, what's up with his name? How can you trust a man named Sly? He's also got creepy eyes—like he's hiding something. He'll steal our treasure."

"You're being overly dramatic, even blaming the poor man for his name. I'm sure it's a nickname. You've got one of those, too, as you keep reminding me. He's a professional instructor, for heaven's sake. You need to trust people. Stop being so paranoid. You're starting to sound like my dad. He never did like accepting help from others."

"Don't talk about Abuelo in the past tense. He's not dead."

"You're right, but he has no choice now but to accept help from the hospital staff."

"You mean pee time with nurse?"

"Enough. I don't want to hear any more of your nonsense or complaints. Sly goes or I don't go."

"Hmph . . ."

"And wipe the snarl off your face. Be polite to him, you understand?"

I slammed the car door and headed toward the dock, ready for combat.

"Need a hand there?" Sly moved to grab my duffel when I reached the boat.

"I got it," I barked.

"Suit yourself, chief." He flicked a cigarette butt onto the ocean.

Dad cleared his throat. "Um. I have to insist. No smoking in front of Fin, please. Or in front of me."

"Yeah, these things will kill you. But something's gotta, right?"

Dad nodded and accepted Sly's hand as he came aboard. He balanced himself, one leg at a time, stepping onto the hull.

"How long you been diving?" Sly asked me.

"Got certified a couple of weeks ago."

"No wonder your dad got me tagging along. Dangerous out here for little kids who ain't got experience." He took off his sunglasses, unmasking dark pits in the depths of his eyes. Worse yet, revealing a long, jagged scar above his left eyebrow. I decided that only the edge of a knife could cause a wound like that.

It all played out in my mind. Captain Sly, terror of the seas, evil pirate, and stealer of treasure. An eye patch covered his scar, and he had a hook in place of his right hand.

He waved around a sword and bellowed, "Surrender the booty!"

Even his tattoos spelled trouble. They weren't the nice kind like Abuelo's anchor. A half-naked woman surrounded by flames decorated his right arm, and a mean-looking sea serpent wound its way around his left biceps.

How could Dad possibly think this guy was okay?

Sly cleared his throat, bringing me back to the present. "I got 'er tanks filled up, enough for two hours. Where ya thinking of heading? I can suggest some real pretty reefs. Water still ain't too clear after the hurricane, but who am I to judge if you folks in a hurry to go out?"

"Fin's in charge of our destination." Dad shot me an exaggerated smile. He had to know I'd be super annoyed at Sly's little kid comment.

"So where to, Fin?" Sly prodded. "Seems your wish is my command." His voice dripped with sarcasm.

Dad kept right on smiling.

I jumped onto the boat and sat in front of the steering wheel before Sly could reach it. "I'll drive. It's my grandfather's boat, and he doesn't like strangers touching it."

"As you wish." Sly grinned in his annoying way. "As long as your daddy allows."

Grrrr . . .

Dad nodded.

I shot arrows at them both with my glare before turning the key to the engine—hard right. First time back on Abuelo's boat, first time without him, and I had to share the ride with this poser.

Not the way I pictured it all going down in my mind. Dad had already found a way to betray me.

Sly leaned over and untied our lines from the wood mooring posts. "You figure out the where-to yet?" He pushed off from the dock. "Guess it don't matter much 'cause ya got me on the clock."

"You'll see," I snapped.

"All right, kid. Makes my job—"

I jerked the boat forward while Sly coiled the ropes into a neat pile.

Ha. Ha. He lost his footing and slipped two feet toward the stern.

"Easy there, cowboy," Sly said.

"He's right, Fin," Dad warned. His knuckles had turned white from holding on to the arms of his seat. "You want to keep driving. Go nice and slow."

I scowled, shifting down to lowest gear, and pointing the bow north. Back to where Abuelo and I meant to search. Before things had so quickly gotten out of control.

I'd come this far convincing Dad to take me out. I had to make things right. No way I'd let Sly ruin it all. I'd find a way around this hiccup in my plans.

After a thirty-minute ride, I cut off the engines and drifted in near Rodriguez Key. It'd been a silent trip, but with the noise of the motors turned off, Sly's nosiness switched on again.

Where are you going? What are you looking for? His questions didn't stop.

I pulled at my hair. *Mind your own business!*

"Dropping anchor here" was my only response.

"You ain't gonna see much of anything out this way." Still, Sly jumped to action, pretending to be all helpful. He crawled up to the bow to toss out the weight and hooked up the Diver Down flag announcing to the world what we'd be doing. "Nice coral reefs close by. I could get us there in five minutes."

Who asked you? I fought to keep my voice steady. Keep my eyes on the prize, as Abuelo often said. "This is where I'd like to dive."

"Suit yourself, kid. But don't complain when you ain't see nothin' but sand."

And hopefully, you ain't see nothing but me disappearing in front of you. Tsk. Tsk.

Quick as I could, I strapped on the BCD vest and tank, along with mask and fins. I balanced the heavy load sitting on the rim of the boat, ready to hit the water. Escape.

"Right behind you." Sly struggled to yank clingy black neoprene around his midsection and zip up his wetsuit.

"Wait for Sly," Dad cautioned.

Not a chance . . . "I need space. To explore on my own."

"Signal if you gots any trouble or equipment issues. Remember, most important sign. You go like this"—he moved his index finger across his throat—"if you got no air."

Thanks for that, Captain Obvious.

Dad shot me a warning look. "Stay—"

My back splashed against the water, drowning out his

words. And, darn it! When my head popped up, Sly was already beside me. He'd be hard to shake.

"Gonna check on the anchor." He motioned beneath the bow. "Don't think it took. Wait here."

Right. I'd show Sly how to do the Slippety—the Slippety Sly Shake. It'd be the only chance I'd get.

The second his head dipped under, I dove down, blowing out of my ears to equalize while my body plummeted.

Down. Down. Down.

I breathed in and out of the regulator, moderating the oxygen, and wiggled my torso imitating a dolphin. My black-and-yellow fins served as propellers, kicking behind me in furious strokes and cutting through current.

Bubbles trailed above as I skimmed grassy beds, passing occasional bursts of corals, their colors muted in the murky water, unsettled from the storm. A school of parrotfish—four, five, six—swam by in a blur of pinks and blues, welcoming me to the hidden depths of their underwater world. I jerked my head in a circular motion. Nothing but fish swam behind.

At last, I was free. Free to explore. Whee . . .

I took my time scouring every inch of ocean bottom, creating a square grid similar to what Great-Grandpapa had logged in his journals. This would be my plan, and I'd log each dive site into my journal—the one Abuelo gave me. I'd continue this way for miles and miles. Plot my coordinates. Chart my destiny. Save Abuelo. Find the family legacy. It all seemed foolproof. Till reality hit. It was a big, big sea with no riches to be found. At least not on this first dive.

An empty air tank later and my confidence whacked down a notch, the boat's hull beckoned from above like a giant bathtub floating. Except there were two. Two boats. Two hulls. More curious than anything I'd seen below.

Sly appeared out of nowhere. He tapped on his watch and his index finger signaled up. The instruction was obvious. Time to go.

The moment I began to ascend, Sly yanked my heel, holding me in place. He made a stop sign with his hand and proceeded to slash through the water in an X stroke.

My mind sped up to match my pulse, skipping into high gear. He couldn't mean X marks the spot, could he? Did he know? Or was he ready to slash me into pieces? I should've known better than returning near the spot where Abuelo's heart took the wrong beat.

A buzzing sound carried down. I craned my neck to study the surface. This had to be the X Sly meant. Engines running above. Props were definitely not something to mess with. They'd be knife blades rotating. Sucking me in and chopping me into bits. Not a nice visual.

I followed his instruction and froze, even down to my breathing.

The other boat had no right invading our dive spot. The Diver Down flag we raised meant all boats had to maintain a three-hundred-foot distance. I studied this. Its presence here wasn't even legal. It was deadly.

The second bathtub glided away on the ocean top.

Once the vessel moved out of sight, Sly loosened his grip and signaled me up again.

Upon breaking through the surface water, Dad treated me to a close encounter with his face. "Find any gold?" He leaned over the edge.

"Shhh. Sly's right behind."

"There you go again. I'm paying him to help you, not steal. You can't go accusing everyone you meet."

"He's not everyone. He's a pirate." Though I had to admit, he did pass up the chance to feed me to the blades. Not that it'd do him much good yet. I had to lead him to the gold before he did away with me.

Dad snickered. "You've got an overactive imagination."

"I know I didn't imagine another boat. Why was there another one next to ours? I saw it from below."

"A diver checking on us. Making sure we were okay."

"But why—"

A splash to my side and Sly's head popped out of the water. "Everything all right?"

"Super!" I climbed on board. "How'd you end up right next to me at the end?"

"Gave you space, but it's what your daddy's paying me for. Stay on your tail."

"Indeed." Dad gave Sly an approving nod.

"That it, kid?" Sly pulled himself up the ladder. "Got another set of tanks filled for one more dive. But like I said before, ain't nothin' down in these parts except for a school of parrotfish and the other boat not minding its business. We can head to the Christ of the Abyss statue. Most popular site this way."

"Been there, and I know where I want to go," I grunted, yanking up the anchor from my post on the bow.

Sly shrugged. "Suit yourself. Your daddy's money."

And Abuelo's treasure, I almost said. How could I get rid of this creep?

11
JAGGED CLUE

A short distance away, I pulled up to a tiny island. The entire length of this deserted key measured less than a football field across. Mangroves barricaded the coastline, their tangle of brown roots plunging into the water like prison bars, warning: KEEP OUT.

I turned to Dad before cutting off the motor. "This is where I want to explore. Less than four feet." I tapped the depth finder. "Easy to walk to shore. On my own . . ." I narrowed my eyes at Sly, sitting in the bow, his eyes hidden behind his mirrored sunglasses.

Dad scratched his chin, examining my face. "Hmm. Time to reapply." He passed me the tube-o-torture.

Groan . . .

He addressed Sly. "This place seem safe to you?"

"Little risk from what I can see."

"You can watch me from the boat," I shot back before cannonballing off the side, and before Dad could find anything else to freak out about.

Bare feet connected with slimy ocean bottom. A mixture of mud and seaweed, sucking me in knee-deep like quicksand. I plowed on, circumventing the natural barriers until discovering a tiny wisp of sand on the far west side to serve as an entrance point.

After a few tries, I yanked my legs from the pool of muck gluing them to the ocean floor and came ashore. Only to find the island had another defensive barrier: hundreds, thousands, of sharp, broken shells lay scattered all over the sand. Spiky minefields guarding its shores. The aroma of ocean scum greeted me when I entered.

I hopped from foot to foot, balancing on tiptoe to avoid the tiny knife blades crunching beneath my toes. Shorebirds gathered around, watching my freakish dance in fascination.

I turned my face into a mask, erasing the stabs of pain, before waving back to Dad and shooting him a thumbs-up sign. For sure, he'd send Sly over with the giant first-aid kit if he knew about the cuts accumulating on my soles.

Pushing back branch after branch, I followed a narrow

trail. The path gave way to roots and chunks of drift-wood as I hiked deeper and deeper into the island. A few more steps and I'd reach the other side.

Ouch!

My toe exploded with pain, banging against a hard object. Another roadblock.

I bent down to examine my foot and my pulse went into overdrive. Nature didn't make this. Only man could craft this corroding piece of steel rail. It was long and almost four inches wide. A thatch of lime-green seagrass and barnacles were attached to the metal. Maybe it had just been tossed ashore in the storm. One thing was sure, it was old. Almost one hundred years old.

The ancient piece of track could only be from Flagler's railroad. How else would this wash out to sea and land in this remote area of the Keys?

My heart sped up, matching the speed of a real-life train racing across the old rail. Treasure could have landed here, too.

I brushed down the rug of seagrass to get a better look.

Yeow!

The jagged edge of a barnacle buried in the seagrass

cut deep into my palm. Blood gushed out, dripping red splotches over the bed of green.

I had to stop the flow. Or . . . I could give in and crawl back to Dad. Surrender to his stupid first-aid kit.

Nah. Not happening. No way I'd give him that level of satisfaction. Control.

I tore off a long sleeve of my rash guard and wrapped it around my hand, tightening it into a knot. At least the pressure would stop most of the bleeding. Buy me a little time—long enough to finish exploring.

I had to try.

Within minutes, one thing did become clear. I wasn't the first to discover this island. After examining every inch of ground, I turned up only discarded beer bottles and food wrappers.

If there was once treasure, whoever beat me here may have found it and left behind a pile of trash when they took off with the loot. Or not. I couldn't stop exploring. The railroad track might only be a clue that I could be closer than ever to finding gold.

Sirena came into view. Sly had taken control of the wheel and was trolling around the key as though tracking my moves to the back side of the island where I stood.

"Let's go!" Dad waved his arms high above his head. I

nodded and he hooked the short dive ladder off his side of the boat.

I waded out and then swam a few yards to the idling boat. When I stepped back on board, Dad's gaze froze on the bloodstained fabric tied around my hand. "Did something bite you?"

"Let me take a look-see." Sly reached toward my hand.

I yanked it out of his reach and unwrapped the cloth, then waved my palm at them both. "A little scratch. Barnacle scrape."

Dad went into semi-hysterical mode, grabbing the first-aid kit. "It's deep. We need to disinfect and bandage."

I'd never hear the end of this . . .

"Relax, Dad."

"I'm not about to relax. Lift your feet. Why are you also trailing blood on the floor?"

"Just a few little cuts." I shrugged. "Shells attacked my feet."

"I let you go alone for fifteen minutes and look at all the trouble you got yourself into," Dad fumed.

I sucked in my breath to accept his sting of antiseptic punishment.

"We need to head back to shore. Sly has another commitment—"

"Then dump him," I hissed in his ear.

Sly pretended he hadn't overheard my comment. "Anything out there that didn't make you bleed, kiddo?"

None. Of. Your. Business. "Some washed-up Cassiopeas," I lied. "We're studying all about jellyfish in science class."

"Huh," Dad said, feigning interest. I'm one hundred percent sure he'd never heard of this species of upside-down jellyfish that could sting if you stepped on it. But now I'd given him one more reason not to step into nature himself.

"We'll drop Sly off at the marina. You sure you can take the boat back to Abuelo's from there?"

I rolled my eyes. "Haven't you seen me driving all day?"

Sly offered his slimy half-smile. "You can always give me a shout on the radio if you get into any trouble. We can send out a rescue party."

"Thanks, Sly. We'll keep that in mind." Dad thought Sly was being sincere, but I knew better. And Sly knew that I knew, which is why he kept it up.

He also knew how eager I was to get rid of him. And maybe he had started to sense why.

12
CATCH A TUBBER

Two weeks passed before I could convince Dad to take me diving again. Abuelo made progress in this time, though not the speaking kind. Still only croaks came out when he opened his mouth.

A few days after Dad and I returned, Abuelo rolled out of the hospital in a wheelchair . . . and rolled right into a rehabilitation facility. What smiley nurse explained to me in baby talk was that this was a place for him to get all better.

I wished it could be so, that I could flick a magic light switch and get him back, strong as he was before. At least I could turn on the switch at his home, now that electricity had been restored. Though I'd choose to live in the dark if it meant getting Abuelo home.

Friday after school—'cause yeah, that resumed—Dad

dropped me off at Abuelo's house. "You can get things organized. I've got a meeting to attend."

Hmm . . . "In the Keys?"

"It'll be quick. I'll stop on my way home and pick up provisions."

"Let me guess. Another flower shirt?"

"Don't get smart with me," Dad snapped. "Remember, I'm only here because of you."

I slammed the passenger door a little harder than necessary before entering Abuelo's house. It welcomed me with its usual cozy embrace as I flicked on the lights. The only sad part was that Abuelo wasn't here to greet me, and we didn't know when he would be back.

Entering the living room was like zapping through a time machine and taking a step back into the guts of an antique sailing ship. Wood-paneled walls displayed fraying nautical flags, antique maps, and a collection of brass artifacts, including the lantern Abuelo had used. Even the smell of salt and mustiness filled the air, adding to the old maritime feeling.

Abuelo's prized possession was mounted above the couch. A blue marlin that measured almost eight feet long. According to Abuelo, it'd been his toughest adversary, putting up a two-hour battle. Its bill, ending in a long, pointy sword, made it easy to see what a fierce fighter he would have been.

The guest room—unofficially "my room," which I liked much more than my room at home—also had cool nautical stuff hanging on every inch of wall space. Framed photos in black and white captured scenes from remote corners of the world. A peek into his Navy days. His mysterious past. To further document his fearless adventures, there was also a picture of Abuelo prying open the jaws of a crocodile with his bare hands.

I beelined it to the kitchen after dropping off my duffel bag. At this moment, my insides growled fierce as a croc—ready to snap and devour anything in sight.

Scanning the cupboards, I found little to work with: one can of beans, two cans of corn, a bag of rice, and a jar of peanut butter. I scooped out some of the sticky goop with two fingers and wolfed it down. The salty-sweet paste stuck to the top of my mouth. At least that'd hold me till I could catch some more protein in case Dad's "provisions" didn't include more than sunscreen and Band-Aids.

Heading toward the dock, I snagged a fishing rod from the shed and rummaged through Abuelo's bottomless tackle box. I chose a slimy green lure with fake eyes and a well-hidden hook. The small metal circle attached to its head made it easy to attach the line.

Abuelo's neighbor, Captain Pete, approached while I made my first casts, far as I could throw. He leaned over the wire fence dividing the two properties. "How's the old man doing, Fin?"

"He's walking on his own and doing lots of exercises. And if he could talk, I'm sure he would scream and shout about how unhappy he is."

Captain Pete shook his bald head. The hair missing on top seemed to be growing on his chin as a generous beard. "Don't you worry yourself. Toughest old salt I know. He'll be good to go in no time."

"I hope so."

Zing. Some line unspooled from the reel and the end of the rod shivered to life, announcing a bite. A huge form floated under the water.

I jumped up and down, pulling back on the pole. "Feels like a giant one." But shoot, judging by the shadow in the water, longer than I was tall, it'd be impossible to bring up.

A large nose and whiskers peeked out of the water.

Captain Pete clapped. "Tubber's back!"

Tubber was their friendly neighborhood sea cow.

"He's been hiding," Captain Pete said. "Thought he didn't make it through the storm."

"Did I hook him?"

"Herbivores of the sea. Wouldn't be attracted to your bait."

Tubber was the color of slate and pear-shaped with a flat rounded tail. "He looks beat up." I pointed at the long gashes extending across the manatee's body.

"Sadly, he had those cuts before. These guys move real slow, often hanging by docks. They take a beating from the props. Boaters don't see them."

"Poor Tubber." I frowned. Truth was, I could've ended up way worse than him if Sly had let me shoot up and meet the random boat that invaded our dive spot. I didn't have the benefit of the manatee's thick elephant-like skin.

"You're gonna lose your bite, you keep yakking. I been getting skunked for days. You got lucky. Don't let it slip away."

"I was sure I caught a Tubber," I snickered, before strengthening my grip to reel in my prize. If only it were so easy to land the real treasure. To keep Abuelo from slipping away from me.

Captain Pete peered at the fish I'd just pulled from the water. "Whatcha got there?"

I grasped the squirmy fish around its midsection with one hand and pried out the hook with the other. Then I held it up for Captain Pete to see. "Is it a keeper?"

"Hmm. Yellowtail. Legal length. Got yourself a fine dinner." He winked. "Say, I came out to tell you that the shipment of lumber Kiki and I ordered the night before he . . ." His words trailed off and he cleared his throat. "Well, to fix our docks. It came in this morning. I can help if you need."

"Thanks, Captain. I'm good."

"Yep. You seem to be doing just fine on your own."

If only Dad could see it this way. We sure didn't need Sly's help. Except maybe to give me a heads-up about the motor blades . . .

"Only one around here bringing up any gifts from the sea. Swing by and pick up the wood when you're ready. In my front yard." He retreated to a tiki structure on the edge of his dock—what remained of it. Half the palm fronds covering the roof had blown off.

"I can return the fish finder Abuelo borrowed," I called after him.

"Take your time. You've clearly got the magic touch when it comes to fishing these waters right now."

I hoped he was right.

Once the fish was scaled, filleted, and rinsed, I threw the meatless carcass into the ocean and made my way back to the kitchen. A sprinkle of blackening spices, a drizzle of olive oil, and "Voilà!" as Abuelo would say, kissing two fingers to the air. Ready to sizzle on his well-heated cast-iron skillet.

Dad walked through the front door just as I flipped the filets. "Mmm. What's that smell?"

"Fresh snapper."

"You're cooking?" Dad looked on in disbelief.

"Lots I can do."

"I see that." Dad placed a brown paper bag on the counter. "Picked up some groceries. Mostly breakfast and frozen stuff. Eggs are all I can cook." He gave me a sheepish grin. "Your mom has us spoiled."

"True. Why is she avoiding us anyways? No text or calls yet."

"You know why. She wants us to have these boys' weekends. Calls it bonding time."

Whatever . . . "Lumber came in. Abuelo ordered it the night before his stroke. To repair his dock. I was thinking we could fix it. Surprise him."

Dad scratched his head. "Great idea, but I'm afraid my skills don't go much beyond screwing shutters. I can hire someone to help us."

"I thought this could be our project. Abuelo has all the tools we need—crowbar, handsaw, jigsaw, drill, hammers."

Dad ran his fingers through his hair. "Guess we can try."

I had him. "And one more thing . . . you think tomorrow when we go out, it can be you and me? Like, lose Sly and stop wasting your money on a babysitter?"

"No more Sly. I promise. I didn't like how he kept giving you a hard time."

Hmph. He noticed? Maybe there was hope for Dad and me, after all.

13
WOT

The next morning at eight o'clock sharp, the doorbell rang, just as I was rushing around getting equipment and supplies ready for today's trip. Dad opened the door to a tall, muscular man with sun-bleached hair. He wore a bathing suit and rash guard. If his clothes didn't already ring alarm bells, the buff wrapped around his neck with red-and-white dive flags confirmed his purpose in life.

I shot daggers at Dad with my eyes. Big harpoon-sized daggers.

He avoided my glare. "This is Max Tinkler. Our dive guide today."

Seriously?

Max extended his hand, giving me no choice but to shake back. He squeezed hard, cracking down on my knuckles. "Your dad tells me you're quite the diver."

Nice buttering up. "That's me." I faked a smile.

At least he looked sort of normal and didn't talk down to me.

"I'm just about ready," I said as the excitement I'd been feeling took a nosedive. What was even the point? With Dad doing his thing—*whoosh*. Fun whizzed out, same way air swishes out from a deflating balloon.

Back in the bedroom, I stared at a photo of Abuelo standing atop a submarine. How did he and Dad even share the same DNA? He'd missed the ocean-loving gene. The thrill for adventure. The only salt flowing through Dad was what Mami called his salt-and-pepper hair.

When I trudged back to the living room, Max wasn't there.

I shot Dad a hopeful look. "Did you send him home?"

"He's out back loading the boat."

"You promised you and I would go out."

"No, I said you wouldn't have to go out with Sly again. I know how much you disliked him. Instead, I hired Max for you. You're welcome."

"I'm supposed to thank you?" My hands balled into fists. "Why do you keep letting strangers in?"

"We've been over this. You know I can't dive."

"Why is that a big deal? I can."

"I'm not putting you at risk, Fin, and I'm not going to apologize for it. That's what a parent is supposed to do—protect his kid. I interviewed Max last night. Runs a local scuba operation. Even knows your grandfather."

"This was your mysterious meeting?"

To break the tension, Dad tried a dorky accent. "Had to make sure he didn't look like a pirate, aye, me hearty?"

Ha. Ha. Not funny . . . "Can we go already?"

An hour later, I dropped anchor in the middle of the ocean. One mile southwest of the key with the railroad track, following the natural flow of currents. I had figured it all out last night in place of sleep and logged my dive and recon trip with Sly into the journal Abuelo gave me to add to the mix.

The biggest difference between my research and Abuelo and Great-Grandpapa's methods was that I didn't even have to use physical maps to figure out new places to check out. Abuelo would frown. He preferred his prehistoric system, but the ocean plotting app I'd downloaded would be so much better. It dealt with all the coordinates on the fly. That and Google. I had geeked out and researched almost every wreck in the Keys. Today could be the day to score big!

Max interrupted my thoughts. "You sure this is where you want to dive?"

"I know, I know, nothing to see here but seagrass and sand."

"Took the words right out of my mouth. But I can take you to a nice spot," Max offered.

"I'm sure you can. Let me guess, Christ of the Abyss?"

Max shrugged. "Just trying to help. Most popular diving in town."

I strapped on my mask. "Nah. Here's good."

Max took his time inspecting all my gauges and gear. "Safety is always good business," he said.

Dad gave him an overenthusiastic grin.

At least Max wasn't sticking his nose in my business. Not yet.

Max checked the depth finder. "Almost sixty feet here. We'll stop to decompress when I signal you. Okay?"

Wow. Max was cooler than I expected. I figured he'd have flagged the fact that as a junior diver I wasn't allowed to go over forty feet deep. Even Abuelo hadn't let me go down this much.

Dad leaned in from his perch on the rim of the boat, a tube of sunscreen in one hand and the other ready to attack.

"Seriously, Dad? You gotta lighten up."

"And you have to start taking this seriously. The sun can be deadly."

"Listen to your dad, kid. Got a bout of skin cancer on my nose. Right here." Max pointed to a scar. It was the friendly kind from a surgeon's blade. Not like Sly's from a knife blade. "Had to get a tumor removed. Not something you want to mess with."

Win for Dad. I took off the mask and smothered on the white gook. "Happy now?"

"Not quite. What's this I heard? Sixty feet? You all are going pretty deep."

"I'll take good care of him," Max said. "Won't leave his side."

Super . . . This wouldn't be a good spot after all if Max had to stay right on top of me because of the extra depth. "You know what? We should move closer to that key over there." I pointed to a speck of land about a mile out. "It'll be shallower, and I'll swim over to explore. Dad lets me do that alone. Right, Dad?"

Dad nodded. "As long as Max accompanies you when

you're diving, I'm good. But I bought you gloves and water shoes to wear." He reached for a canvas tote bag, pulling his version of a magic rabbit out of a hat. "Ta-da. This way you won't get cut again."

I wanted to roll my eyes, but I had to hand it to him. "Actually, that's great, Dad. Thanks." I would be happy not to get sliced and diced next time I went ashore.

Dad smiled as I brought the motors back to life.

Max stood behind the captain's chair, holding on to the rail. "What are you looking for anyway? Not much out this way."

I knew there would be questions sooner or later . . . I had to shake him off. "Nature stuff. Shells. Driftwood. Things for my science class. I like to collect stuff. Solo. You know, being one with nature, getting my chi on." Hee-hee. Sounded good, anyways. Mami talked about this hokey finding your life-energy thingy she'd learned in her yoga classes, along with moves called Happy Baby, Downward Dog, and—yeesh!—Corpse Pose.

"Got you. I'll give you space. When I was your age, I used to love exploring. My pop was a fisherman. We grew up dirt poor. Didn't have a skiff of my own, of course, so I'd tag along with Pop's crew any chance I could. Always dreamed I'd find treasure hidden on one of the smaller keys and become rich. Silly dream, right?"

I swallowed hard and let out a nervous giggle. "Treasure? Out here? You must have been really little."

Max studied my face. "About your age, in fact. How old are you?"

"Twelve. When did you first get certified?" I had to change the subject.

"Later than you. I was eighteen. Been diving for ten years. Working the biz for five."

"Dad said you know my grandfather?"

"What's with the interrogation?" Dad interrupted.

"It's okay." Max smiled. "Everyone knows Kiki around here. Kind of a legend bringing up big game fish, and one of the regular divers before, before . . . it's too bad about his—"

"He'll get better," I cut in. I'd make sure of it.

"Strange thing about Kiki though, he always liked to go out alone. Never wanted anyone along. Kind of like you."

Another gulp . . . "Yep, take after my grandpa."

"Can get dangerous when you don't use the buddy

system in diving. Went out with a novice diver once and . . ." Max pursed his lips and took an index finger to his throat. His eyes blazed to match the sinister slicing motion he made. "Good thing I was around to help him."

Now Dad seemed to want to change the subject, as this was his worst nightmare.

"I'll tell you what," he said. "Starting to get used to this. Real pretty out here, especially with the water flat as glass today. Kind of an aquarium when you look down. You can see little yellow-and-white-striped fish darting around. And look"—he pointed—"a blue one."

"Sergeant Majors," I said. "And a blue tang." I was grateful the water had settled on the Atlantic side in the few weeks since I'd gone out with Abuelo and we'd needed Captain Pete's fish finder. At least I'd be able to see more than the blurry underwater landscape that greeted me when I'd gone down with Sly.

"Some folks call this paradise," Max said, circling a hand to the sky. "For me, it's a way to make a living. Diving capital of the world here—lots of tourists coming in. Slow now, post-Irma, so it's good to get a gig today. 'Preciate it."

I'd had it with the small talk. "I'm out." My body splashed into the water.

"Signal if you need me," Max yelled after me.

Different babysitter, same result. Except for the two cockle shells I pulled out of the pocket of my swim trunks—fake proof I'd been gathering specimens for a science project—the island exploration was a big WOT (Waste of Time).

Next we went back to the sixty-foot spot, and it proved to be bust number two. I could almost hear Abuelo going on and on about the limits of technology. Sure was true. The ocean plotting app got the WOT rating. Even with access to nautical charts and GPS plotters, there was no simple way to find this treasure. The app didn't come with AI to make the educated guesses Abuelo said he'd made throughout the years.

Worse yet, besides dealing with Max right on my tail, little Squidwards decided to trail behind me, stirring up a wave of bad memories of my ink-splattering in fifth-grade science. They propelled themselves across the depths, their squishy arms dragging behind them—ten to be exact, eight arms and two longer tentacles. I'd never forgotten after having to stretch them out and count them. Right after my science teacher slapped dissecting pans with goopy specimens on our desks back in fifth grade, following lunch break.

"Make your first incisions," she'd commanded, and I had gagged from the smell of formaldehyde as I dug into the squid's body using a tiny scalpel. When I reached the lower part, SPLISH! Cut too deep. This was the terrible part of the memory. The squid burst open like a volcano spewing black, sticky ink everywhere. And over my lab partner and fifth-grade crush, Patty May. She'd insisted on getting a new lab partner and never sat next to me again.

"Fin. Fin. You in there?" Dad jabbed. "Ready to skedaddle? Grab a bite?"

I grimaced. "Not hungry. Don't think I ever want to eat."

Max chuckled. "Should've caught us some of the calamari swimming all around us, eh?"

Ugh. I hated him more than ever for intruding on Dad and me.

14
DIP SEA SURPRISE

Another month passed with eight more dive spots checked off my list, yet the only worthwhile clue logged into my journal was the piece of railroad track I'd found during the first outing with Sly. Weekday trips to visit Abuelo at the rehab center, along with weekend trips back and forth to the Keys with Dad, became the routine.

Abuelo's progress was slow, his mood grim. But at least he was starting to speak.

Saturday mornings down at Abuelo's house, Max rang the doorbell by eight o'clock. He'd become background noise—just part of our routine. Two dives a day, back-to-back, and then he'd walk away with his wallet full simply for babysitting me.

One Saturday in October, it wasn't only the

temperature that dipped to what the weather guys were calling "unseasonably cold" and gloomy.

Dad's mood had also taken a dip, but I had something special in mind to liven things up.

So far that morning, the ocean had matched the forecast—cold and depressing. Nothing but disappointment on our first dive. But as we were closing in on the second destination, the ocean turned a bright shade of turquoise contrasting against the dreary gray skies.

As I powered the boat toward the surprise I had in mind, Max nudged me from behind. "You've been going for over six nautical miles, Fin. If you reveal where you're heading, maybe I can help direct you if you're lost."

"I got this," I said, and soon shifted to idle speed as a one-hundred-foot skeletal pyramid of a tower rose into view. Painted blood red, it shone through wisps of fog drifting over the sea.

"Ah, the old Carysfort Reef Lighthouse," Max said, adding a creepy inflection to his voice. "Gotta be careful though. Current around here, compliments of the Gulf Stream, is unforgiving."

From my research I knew he was right. I imagined the

area as a sort of cemetery of ships, but the breathtaking blue of the water made it seem the opposite of scary.

"The lighthouse is named after a Royal Navy battleship which ran aground in the late seventeen hundreds," Max explained. "It's considered the most dangerous reef in the Keys."

Shoot. I wasn't planning on advertising that last part of its history.

Dad didn't miss a beat. "And if it's so treacherous, we're coming here why? Don't get what you expect to find here, Fin."

I narrowed my eyes. "A little fun. Thought it'd be cool to hunt down a ghost. Rumor has it the lighthouse keeper, Captain Johnson, died here. They say you can hear his spirit moaning and at times even his skeleton floating over the water. Woo-ooo-ooo."

Dad shot Max a questioning look.

"All true." He nodded. "Not to mention ghosts from all the other wrecks—over sixty have been recorded here."

"They say . . . even a ship named *Guerrero*," I continued. "It sailed from Africa on its way to Cuba carrying over five hundred slaves. Forty-one of them drowned as the ship hit a reef and sank. Thought to happen right around this spot."

"The African slave trade is the cruelest part of Caribbean history," Dad said, and frowned. "All those lost souls. Swiped from their homes and families. Their freedom stolen."

Wicked. Evil. Those were the words that came to mind. "Abuelo told me about the *Guerrero* a long time ago. When we see him next week I wanted to tell him we visited this place, since it has Cuba mixed in, just like—"

Shoot. I barely stopped myself short of spilling the beans.

"Just like our family," Dad finished my sentence and gave me a wink. "I'm not one to believe in the supernatural, but don't think I want to stick around here."

"Ghosts only appear after nightfall, Dad. I'm going in. Less than four feet deep on most parts of the reef. No risk of the physical kind," I snickered. "I'll wade in and snorkel. Alone." I reached for my fins but decided to leave them behind. With it being so shallow, I didn't want to risk harming the delicate corals.

Dad grunted. "Doesn't sound like a good idea."

"Please, can't you just roll with it?"

To my surprise, Dad did exactly that. "All right, Fin." He took a long sip of coconut water and passed me my mask. "The better to see what dangers lurk in the deep . . . Muah hah hah."

Corny but it cracked me up. I could definitely deal with this version of Dad for keeps.

Danger, however, was lurking right there as I stepped off the dive ladder and submerged my body into the chilly water. Translucent creatures with stringy blue and purple tentacles trailing off their sail-shaped bodies floated near the surface.

Portuguese men-of-war. Yikes! My heart responded with an extra thump. I froze and didn't go under.

Best to steer clear. Waaay clear.

"Careful with the jellies," Max shouted. "They like to hang out near this reef for some reason. Warding off invaders. Also—"

Too late. It became obvious what he was about to warn of next.

Sharks!

Babies, though. And nurse sharks—the more harmless type. I counted three, no, four. They skimmed across shallow fields of bright-colored corals, minding their own business.

"Fin, get out!" Dad screamed, pointing at the small school around me. "Max, can you grab him?"

Max dipped a cautious toe in the water before he plunged neck deep. It was clear he wasn't thrilled to be told to go swim with predators.

Then, *swish* . . .

An attacker crept up from behind and lunged at him with one evil tentacle. I watched it all play out faster than I could open my mouth and alert him.

My babysitter screamed and gripped the back of one of his thighs. Victim of the venomous sting of a man-of-war.

He hightailed it back onto the ladder, back on the boat, still shrieking while bending to hold his leg. He huffed and puffed and shouted to Dad, "My bag! Pass my gear bag. I've got vinegar. Always bring some along in case of . . . this."

As Dad hurried to get Max's bag, he ordered me out of the water. "You're done, Fin. Out of there this instant! This spot felt cursed from the start. We're heading back."

No major complaints from me. I was happy to leave the lighthouse to these predators . . .

But as I swung onto the boat, I had a twisted thought: This could be it. A reason for Max to bail. A way to shake babysitter number two, so it'd be down to just a cooler version of Dad and me.

That version of Dad was short-lived.

Early the same evening, Mami, with Ratón shoved into a purse, arrived to surprise us. Her dress was fancy—yellow and bright. High heels matched the same sunny shade, along with the hibiscus flower pinned in her black hair. Even rat dog had a matching yellow ribbon band stuck between the pointy ears on his head.

I gave Mami a peck on the cheek. "Flip-flops are more the uniform in the Keys."

"Stop teasing her. She looks beautiful. Always does." Dad gave her a dopey smile. "Too pretty to keep inside. Let's go out to dinner and celebrate her visit. There's something important I need to discuss with you."

Uh-oh.

The bad news was written all over Dad's face when we stepped into Mer-Man's, a local fish joint, and one of the first restaurants he and I had found open post-hurricane apocalypse. Ocean-blue walls were covered in fishing nets and kitschy nautical décor, heavy on the mermaid theme. Dad ushered us into a booth, ready to launch into one of his lectures.

I had a pretty good idea of what he was about to say, and it wasn't one bit of a cool-dad move. If I could ignore him long enough, distract him, maybe I'd get him to forget about it.

I hunched down and played with my phone.

Dad cleared his throat. "Fin, look up. We need to talk."

"Huh. What?"

"I've been supporting you—"

"Check out the photo I took of the haunted lighthouse."

"Nice." Dad nodded. "Back to what I was saying . . . I've supported—"

"This one is better." I turned my screen.

"*Pero* stop interrupting your papi," Mami said. "*Presta atención.*"

Groan . . .

Dad began again. "Fin, we've been chasing this dream of yours for weeks—and now you've even got me watching you swim with sharks and those iridescent stinging things."

Yikes. This was not information that needed to be shared with Mami.

Her hands flew to the sides of her mouth. "*¿Tiburones?* What do you mean you swam with sharks?"

A waitress popped up to our booth. Her hair, dyed green and twisted in tiny braids, resembled strands of seaweed.

"Thank you!" I'd never been so happy to have my glass filled with water.

She smiled and dropped plastic-covered menus on the table. "Holler when you're ready."

"Wait!" Mami called after her. "You got any of those fried Keys balls to start and calamari?"

The waitress gave Mami a look like she was growing two heads, and then she smiled.

"You mean conch fritters? Calamari and conch are always available. House specialties, along with the Key lime pie—graham crust and right amount of tart."

"Yes. Send the critters and calamari out first, please. I'm starving."

"Mami, if you order calamari, I swear I'll puke."

"Charming." Mami scrunched her face and turned to the waitress. "Skip the squid."

"Fresh order of critters it is." The waitress winked. "Back in a bit."

Dad was out of patience. As soon as she'd left, he

slapped his hand down on the table so that the ice in our drinks jiggled. "Face it, Fin. It's time you accept the truth. There's no way you can find this treasure. You could search for the rest of your life just like Dad and my grandfather, and still not find it."

"I can—"

"It's not healthy, son. We need to make sure your abuelo forgets this obsession of his which he's passed on to you. Help him find peace. You both need it."

"Why are you the only person in the family who can't believe?"

"Someone's got to be practical," Dad said, scanning the menu. "Ready to order?"

"No! I'm not ready to stop trying. How can you give up on the family legacy? Give up on helping Abuelo?"

"My legacy is different. It's about stability. Earning an honest living. Being a good provider for you and your mom."

"Así es." Mami patted his hand.

"But all I've asked you for is to drive me down and take me diving. And now you can't even do this."

"How about a little gratitude, Fin? I've footed the bill for gas, for your diving partner, for your Band-Aids and sunblock. I've been more than generous indulging you."

I laid on my best pout. "Can I go out at least one more time? I still have a few more places I want to check out. Pleeease."

"You think it's going to make a difference? There's always going to be one more spot. I can't keep coming down and paying for Max indefinitely. If he even wants to go out again . . ."

"I never asked for a babysitter."

Dad took a slow sip of water. "I'm sorry."

The waitress poked her head back into our booth. "Did you choose?"

I slunk back in my seat. What choice did I have? Dad had ended our deal.

"Sorry, I lost my appetite," I said.

Shell-shaped bells rattled as the door to Mer-Man's closed behind us. On the other half of the salmon-colored building, the storefront sign read *Dip Sea Laundromat* in handcrafted squiggly letters.

A man wearing all black leaned against the wall of its entrance, blowing out wisps of smoke. When he brought the cigarette to his mouth, his arm flexed so the sea serpent decorating his left biceps twisted into view.

I'd seen that tattoo before. This man was no stranger.

Dad kept an arm around Mami as they strolled along, buried in conversation. I dodged around them, bolting to the car in stealth-mode. Our parking spot, two spaces down, allowed a safe distance to spy.

The doors to Dip Sea pushed open. "Sylvester, come help."

Sylvester? I had a hard time picturing Slippety Sly as Sylvester, but who else could it be? Ha! He'd been given a stuffy birth name. Same as me.

"Sylvester." The woman popped into view. Her hair, white as a bleached sand dollar, gave away her years. She pushed her way through the entrance, balancing on a cane. "The basket. I can't—"

"I'll get it, Nana." Sly's tone was gentle. He put out his cigarette, waving away the smoke, and escorted his grandmother to a car. The jalopy, tired and rusted with age, hardly seemed safe. He banged against the passenger door, prying it open, before holding out a hand and helping his grandmother into the seat. Then he closed the door for her, the way Mami always told me a gentleman should. "I'll go grab your clothes."

Mami and Dad approached my hiding spot, their voices carrying over the air. At the sound, Sly swung his head in our direction, locking in with my stare.

Crap. Outed. I had no right to be sneaking a glimpse into his private life—his very normal private life. He had a grandmother who relied on him. I had never bothered to ask about his family.

He narrowed his eyes and shook his head, giving me a disappointed scold.

I deserved this and more. After all, I had sold him out. Proclaimed him a pirate, and judging by his beat-up ride, he probably needed the gig with Dad and me real bad.

15

GOLD SEAWEED ROAD

I tossed and turned that night in my room at Abuelo's house. Guilt swept over me. Same as the waves crashing outside my window, rushing over my sheets. Soaking them with seawater. Or was it sweat?

Dreams. Reality. It wasn't quite clear.

My bed began swaying. Side to side.

I looked over the edge, clinging on to the bedding. The rug underneath churned to life, becoming a dark gray sea. Wavy crests rolled in with a surge of current. They intensified with rage until mighty breakers built up, crashing against the wood frame.

My body shook out of control, drenched head to toe in salt spray. I bent my legs to my chin, shivering from the slap of the angry sea.

The ceiling tore open with a crackling force. A funnel

cloud shot down, creating a vortex. Twisting on top of me. With every rotation, it was sucking me closer to its core.

Closer to where I could see this was no ordinary cloud. Scales became visible. A dark green body coiled into rings.

Snake? Dragon?

A beast. A monster I'd seen before in dreams.

No. This one was real. Real as the evil sea serpent tattooed on Sly's arm. Payback. He'd sent it after me.

It opened its jaw wide, revealing fangs and rows of sharp teeth. The smell of rotting fish and algae exploded from within.

I could no longer breathe.

The tail, ending in long pointy fins, wrapped around my neck. Squeezed and squeezed. Slimy snake-like scales pressed down, sucking the final air out of me.

I swam into a pit of darkness. Death?

Nothing made sense. My mind continued to fight for release, clawing through the black cape that was drowning me in nothingness. I managed to break free. Tear away the misery surrounding me.

Black turned gray. Gray turned blue. Skies and oceans of turquoise blue. Puffy, cotton-shaped clouds floated amid this perfect blue, setting me adrift. Hugging me with happiness. Peace. Heaven?

Rays of golden light shot down through a cloud and the image of a man appeared. Illuminated by sunshine, goodness glowed around him. He waved. The instruction clear, I followed, no longer suffocating in fear.

Transparent water rose around me till it leveled off shoulder-deep. I swam, slicing through a gentle current. With each stroke, I inched closer and closer until I could get a better look at the man's face.

Abuelo?

Thoughts swirled inside my head. Nothing made sense. Was I trapped in a dream? Had I let Abuelo down? Let the sea serpent get the best of me?

I stopped to examine the man's face, searched for the faded anchor tattoo.

It wasn't there.

The man looked so much like Abuelo. But no. Not the same.

He waved me over again. "Keep going. I'll show you the way. Follow me. Follow me."

A large patch of seaweed threaded together at his feet, turning into a thick carpet. The sun's rays shot an electric charge onto the brown algae, making it glint against the turquoise-blue water. It dazzled as if spun of gold before shaping itself into a long path extending on and on in front of me.

Abuelo-ish man turned so I could only see his back. He floated above the golden seaweed road. A ghost. Inching his way forward, he continued to beckon me.

I lifted myself out of the water and tiptoed behind him. Humming. I came up with a silly version of the famous song from *The Wizard of Oz* as I skipped along. (Yes, I actually skipped.)

Follow the gold seaweed road.
Follow the gold seaweed road.
Follow, follow, follow, follow,
follow the gold seaweed road.
We're off to find a treasure,
a treasure that no one knows.

The man kept guiding.
I follow, follow, followed.
My cringey tune played on endless repeat. Ah! Why didn't this dream come with a mute switch?

For miles and miles, I leaped over twists and turns of golden algae with the grace and strength of a ballet dancer.

Nothing changed for a long while until we reached a tower. A guiding beacon. A few feet northeast of it, we arrived at a shipwreck.

Abuelo-ish man stopped and pointed down. The water, crystal clear as a looking glass, made it easy to see every shape buried beneath its surface. An old cannon lay on the ocean bottom, a deadly remnant of the wreck.

BANG!

Recognition flashed inside my head. I'd seen this dive site before—at least pictures of it after obsessively researching all of the big shipwrecks in the Keys.

We were near Elbow Reef. The *City of Washington* wreck. This old schooner turned steamship built in the late eighteen hundreds had fallen to its watery grave here. The funny thing is the ship had ties to Havana, same as Abuelo's treasure.

During the Spanish-American War, it transported troops to Cuba, years before it had struck the reef. Now schools of fish, not soldiers, made a home of it. Good thing I even read all the history part.

Abuelo-ish man trekked on. I charted his course as I

would on a map, committing his steps to my brain like computerized GPS coordinates. By footstep two hundred twenty-two, he held out a palm, coming to a stop.

As part of the weird dream sequence, two dolphins jumped out of the water in opposite directions. They formed a synchronized arc behind him before diving back down, out of sight.

"This is your final stop." He pointed beneath him. "What you've been searching for. Use it to help another."

Before I could see for myself, tell him thank you, goodbye, nice to meet you, anything . . . saliva slopping on my face along with the sound of Mami's voice jolted me awake.

"*Despierta, mi amor.* I've got your favorite *pastelitos.*"

Arf! Ratón now invaded my personal space with his bad breath.

I shot up from bed and out the door, my heartbeat racing ahead of me.

"*Bueno,* you woke up hungry. Not even a good morning, a hug, a hello?"

"Sorry, Mami. Got to tell Dad."

Mami chased after me. "*¡Pero, que bien!* The two of you. You're inseparable now."

In Abuelo's chair, Dad lowered his newspaper and

peered over his spectacles. "What's all the fuss? Why are you running a marathon this early?"

"I know where it is. I know!"

"Yes, right here." Mami extended a tray filled with Cuban pastries. *"Oye, como tiene hambre."* She winked at Dad. "And how sweet, he wanted to share them with you."

"No, I'm not hungry." I brushed the pastries aside. "I mean, thanks, but later. It's the treasure. I found it."

"¿Qué? What do you mean? Your papi told you last night not to search anymore." Mami scrunched her forehead.

"I know where to find it, though. I do."

"I admire your confidence, but how do you expect to do this?" Even through his glasses, I could see Dad's doubtful scowl. "I already told you I'm not going out anymore."

"It came to me in a dream. Hold on. I can prove it." I reached under Abuelo's coffee table and picked up his album of family memories from the bottom shelf. After flipping through pages, I stopped to point at a black-and-white image. "There." I remembered seeing this photo and admiring the big game fish. Abuelo sat next to his dad on a boat, a huge swordfish displayed like a trophy across their laps. It was him, the man in my dream!

"Great-Grandpapa." My voice cracked. "He showed me the way. I met him. I met him. He came to me."

"Sounds like quite a dream." Mami walked over to the kitchen. "They can feel so real."

"But they're not." Dad said, rising from his seat to follow her.

"*¿Más cafecito?*" Mami automatically refilled the empty mug in his hand.

"It's true. He showed me the way to the treasure!"

"And just how did he do this?" Dad gave an exaggerated eye roll. "A crystal ball?"

I opened my mouth to answer, then immediately zipped it closed. I couldn't exactly tell Dad I believed I should follow a gold seaweed road. He'd take me to see a head doctor instead of the treasure.

"Poo. Poo. Don't listen to your father, Fin." Mami gave me a lopsided grin. "I believe loved ones can visit us in our dreams. They watch over us like the angels."

"There's one way to find out. Let's go!"

16
FINITO

Within minutes, it became clear. Dream or no dream, there'd be no convincing Dad.

"Not going. Not happening. Not today." He stopped short of "ever," but the implication hung in the air. He'd already done his time. No more treasure.

"*Mucho ruido y pocas nueces,*" Mami tried to explain.

I rolled my eyes. Another of her annoying Spanish sayings to tell me I'd done too much talking without showing results. "But why don't you let me prove I know the way?"

"*¡Finito!*" Dad's hand crashed down on the coffee table.

It felt like a punch to the gut. This marked the end of the golden seaweed road. No going back.

I ran to my room and slammed the door, locking away the anger boiling inside me so I wouldn't explode. Why couldn't Mami and Dad understand the treasure was the only way to save Abuelo—to help him see that he hadn't wasted his life looking for something that didn't exist? Did they not care about him as much as I did?

A half hour later, Dad knocked on the door. "Open up, Fin. No more time to lose. I've got a consolation prize for you."

"Unless you changed your mind about taking me out to rescue the gold, go away."

"Instead of this make-believe fantasy, I've got a tangible way to help your grandfather."

I balled up a shirt and threw it at the door. "How else could you possibly help Abuelo?"

"It's your idea."

I stayed silent. Mine?

"Come out. Let's knock out the deck repairs before we head home. Meet me out back."

He had me. I slinked my way to the patio, tracing the sound of his retreating footsteps.

"Got everything organized and researched." Dad had arranged the lumber, hammer, saw, deck screws, and other tools in perfect little rows. Instead of a construction zone, the area looked sterilized, neat, more like the hospital's ICU.

"The perfect father-son project." Mami walked out with a pitcher and glasses. "Made you boys lemonade. It's hot out here."

Yeah. My insides still simmered. I picked up a hammer and banged a loose slat into place on the deck full force.

⚓

Before nightfall, Mami popped out again. "¡*Que maravilla!*" she exclaimed.

"The deck or the sunset?" Dad wiped the beads of sweat from his forehead.

"Both." Mami grinned and gazed at the fire painted across the sky. "When did you get to be so handy, Papito? We'll have to put your new skills to use at our house. Too bad you hired roofers to fix our hole."

Dad laughed. "Fin took the lead today. Quite the handyman, this boy."

"Told you I knew how to use a drill." I revved up the screw gun in my hand for effect.

"Getting late," Mami yelled above the noise. "We need to head back to Miami. Work and school tomorrow."

Dad took pictures of the finished deck with his

phone. "We'll visit your abuelo and surprise him. This will cheer him up."

After Dad got home from work the next day, we went to the rehab facility. We signed in with the receptionist, then headed toward Abuelo's wing. At the nurses' station, a male nurse, wearing scrubs the color of midnight, sat behind the desk, eyes fixed on his cell. A discarded take-out container was in front of him, infusing the air with the smell of old cheese.

Dad cleared his throat. "We'd like to see Enrique Román, please."

I stared at the man's nameplate while he continued to peck and swipe at his screen: *Charles Smiles*. I couldn't think of a worse name for him.

"Visiting hours are nearly over. He's probably sleeping," he finally said in a sour tone.

"I'd be asleep, too, if I had to hang here," I whispered to Dad.

The nurse narrowed his eyes, making it obvious he'd overheard.

"Enrique's used to the outdoors," Dad explained. "Salt

air and sunshine. Not the type of man who does well confined to a bed."

"Right." The nurse kept his lips pursed and shoved his phone into a pocket. "Room 222." He pointed down a dimly lit hall where the smell of pine-scented disinfectant was overwhelming.

When we stopped in front of the door, I realized it was the same number of steps I had counted in my dream. Coincidence?

We pushed it open and flipped on the light switch, but even with the overheads on, the room remained gray—a cold fluorescent gray. Dad said Abuelo was fortunate to have a private room, but the room always made me depressed. Not a single photograph or painting hung on the wall to liven up the space. I wished I could bring Abuelo's colorful collection of nautical flags or his big fish trophy. Anything to fill the emptiness.

Mami walked to the row of windows past Abuelo's bed and opened the shades. "Let's let in some light."

Nice try, Mami. Except it was cloudy and dreary. With dusk settling, it would be pitch dark outside within minutes.

The TV set blared, but Abuelo's head lay to the side,

eyes shut tight. This wasn't like Abuelo. He didn't even have a TV at his home. Called them "idiot boxes."

Worry kicked in. "Is he okay?"

"Just resting," Mami said.

"How do we turn off the TV?" Dad asked.

I pulled out the remote hidden beneath the sheets and pressed a button. The room became engulfed in silence. Only Abuelo's snores could be heard.

"Abuelo . . . Abuelo," I called.

"Enrique." Mami patted his hand.

"Kiki," I whispered.

"Kiki, wake up," Mami tried.

Her high-pitched plea must've done the trick. Abuelo opened his eyes and stared around the room. His pupils registered confusion.

"We're all here to visit—*tu familia*." Mami spoke gently. She opened her purse and a head popped out. "Even Ratón."

Abuelo stayed silent, eyes darting back and forth between Dad and me.

"We brought something to cheer you up." Dad pulled out his phone and showed him the photos of the deck.

Abuelo nodded slowly. "Doubt I'll ever get to see it," he croaked.

"That's not a good attitude. Of course you will." Mami's encouraging tone matched her big smile.

I had to come up with something else to liven up Abuelo without telling him all about our treasure hunt. Because, what if I never got to the gold? That'd be a worse disappointment. Get his hopes up—then, bang! Nothing. Without Dad taking me out, ending our hunt, it was a reality I might score a goose egg.

"*Sirena,*" I blurted instead. "I'm taking good care of her for you. Been running the engine. Keeping her in shape."

He grunted and turned to stare out the window.

Not a good sign. If he didn't perk up at the mention of *Sirena,* he'd given up for sure.

He was losing hope. I was losing time. I had to get the treasure. And fast. It could be the only chance for recovery he had.

Lying in bed that night, my mind went into overdrive. I had to come up with a way to help Abuelo. I couldn't count on another rescue team swooping down in a helicopter. I couldn't count on Dad.

I looked at the walls of my room for inspiration. I

didn't have the cool photos and nautical stuff hanging in Abuelo's house spurring me on to adventure. Instead, the pillows, curtains, posters in my room screamed of the generic "boy" theme Mami had chosen for me when I was little: Sports. Soccer, baseball, basketball, and football, to be exact. The one sport not pictured on my kid-sized bedspread was the one I actually liked. Swimming.

At least I had a few diving magazines piled on my desk along with a library book about Mel Fisher. I'd read he was one of the greatest treasure hunters of the sea who discovered the *Atocha* wreck—a Spanish galleon dripping with gold and emeralds.

The coolest part was that this ship had ties to Cuba. It sailed from the port of Havana—its last stop—before embarking on its intended voyage to Spain. All shipwrecks scattered around the Keys seemed to have this Cuban-linked heritage. Same as the train wreck treasure. Same as me.

I remembered standing in front of the Southernmost Point monument in Key West when I was younger. Mami had snapped about twenty pictures. The big concrete buoy-shaped marker even had hand-painted letters declaring ninety miles to Cuba. From this point, it was closer to Havana than to Miami, which was twice that distance.

Strong winds and waves had crashed *Atocha* against a reef, sinking it only twenty miles from Key West. The wreck played hide-and-seek for three hundred and fifty years till Fisher could find it.

He'd used all sorts of fancy equipment to dig up his loot, including a super high-tech-sounding proton magnetometer. It detected objects on the ocean bottom in what I'm sure was a way more precise way than Captain Pete's simple fish-o-meter.

Me, before I could become one of the greatest treasure hunters who ever lived and rescue Abuelo from a life of defeat, I had to stick to the map from my dream since my tech app had proved a WOT. But first, I had to figure out how to even get back to the Keys. Pronto.

Swimming there wasn't an option, so with Dad quitting on me, I'd need a way to make the trip on my own. Get me some wheels. I grabbed my cell off the desk and launched an internet search. Googling was becoming another favorite sport.

Fifteen minutes later, I'd come up with a plan. Tomorrow would be the day I'd execute Mission: Save Abuelo.

17
MISSION ORDERS

Stuffing down eggs, bacon, and—the best part—Mami's fresh-baked banana bread for breakfast, I fought to keep my chill. Pretend everything was normal. The chocolate chips hidden in the dough oozed in my mouth while I rehearsed the plan in my head.

Dad popped his head into the kitchen. "Your mom's driving you in today," he said. He wore a suit and tie and held a briefcase in one hand, car keys in the other. "Early meeting at the office."

"Ay, ay, ay. Let me finish getting ready." Mami rushed off, yanking rollers out of her hair.

"Take your time," I called after her. Things were already playing out my way. One thing I could count on was Mami getting me to school a few minutes late.

At eight o'clock on the nose, or oh-eight-hundred as Abuelo would say to kick off one of our adventures, Mami pulled up to the end of the car line outside school.

"Ugh, it's bad today. I'll get off here and run in. Think I can make it before they mark me late. Don't want to get a tardy."

Mami smiled. "How responsible of you."

"I know, right?" I grabbed my backpack—aka my mission pack—and pushed open the door. I was doing the responsible thing for sure . . .

"Have a great day." She blew a kiss. *"Te quiero."*

"I sure will." I watched her car turn the corner before dodging out of sight of the crossing guard and heading in the opposite direction of the entry gates.

I had it all figured out. Quick walk to the Metrorail train. Metro to take the bus to the southern end of Miami in Florida City, then, transfer to bus three-oh-one down to the Keys. After an hour's ride—maybe more with extra stops—I'd be close enough to walk to Abuelo's house.

Mami and Dad wouldn't even know I was gone. I

had until at least three in the afternoon. Long enough to secure the treasure. And long enough to get back to school before pick-up time. The plan was foolproof.

Boarding the bus after completing the Metro ride, I kept my chin down and face hidden underneath a baseball cap while I swiped the bus pass I'd bought at the station.

The driver gave me the once-over. "Aren't you supposed to be in school, young man?" Her tone was no-nonsense.

Busted. Heat crept up my face as I figured out what to tell her. I chose not to lie. "I have to go down and help my grandpa today. He's very sick and doesn't have anyone else who cares about him."

She offered one of those sad little smiles I'd been getting from all Abuelo's nurses before she waved me on. I scuttled to the last row and slumped into a seat, jamming in my earbuds.

Thirty minutes and two granola bars later, my phone rang. Mami's number popped up on the caller ID. Shoot. Why would she call me if she thought I'd be in class?

I let it go to voicemail.

Beep after beep announced a series of texts coming in.

Mami: Where are U? Why aren't U at school?

Double shoot.

Mami: Pick up the phone. Answer me.
Mami: Are U OK? I'm calling the police.

I don't know if she called the police. I do know that she called Dad. Within seconds, a new text popped up.

Dad: Report back to us at once.

I ignored the messages, putting the phone on mute. A little longer to go. I had to stick to the plan.

After what turned into a two-hour bus ride, followed by a twenty-minute walk in the heat, I arrived at Abuelo's house. A man sat on the front steps dressed in a suit and tie.

Crap! Not any man.

Dad!

One thing I'd learned, it was better to launch the offensive than defend against one. "What are you doing here?"

Dad leaped up. "Question is, why are you here, over sixty miles away from home?" His voice trembled with rage to match the fire shooting from his eyes. "Or do I need to even ask?"

"How did you know I was here and not in school?"

"You're not the only one who's clever. Once the school sent an email to alert us you were AWOL, it wasn't hard to guess what you were up to."

Oh.

"You've got a lot of answering to do. You put yourself at risk and made me leave work to chase you down."

"But you wouldn't bring me," I said, as a crushing wave of sadness swept over me. "I begged and begged. Abuelo's going to die if I don't cheer him up with the treasure."

"You're being dramatic," he said, but I could hear in his voice that he was starting to get as emotional as I was.

"No, I'm not. Did you see how depressed he was last night?"

We both went silent. I wiped the tears off my cheeks.

Dad handed me a tissue from a packet he carried in his pocket.

"Did you hitchhike down here?" he asked.

"No!" I said. I told him how I'd done it. He looked horrified—and maybe a little impressed.

Then he rubbed his chin. "Truth is, I'm worried about my dad, too. But it doesn't excuse your running off. I know you were planning to take the boat out and go diving by yourself. The bus is bad enough, but do you know how dangerous that would have been? You could have been killed."

"Now you're being the dramatic one."

"We're not going to resolve this arguing." Dad threw his hands up in the air. "What's it going to take to get this foolish treasure hunt off your mind once and for all?"

"If you take me out to find it—one last time—I promise I'll never bring it up again. Never ever."

Dad paced back and forth. Anger faded from his face as though he was walking it off. "I'm trying to be patient. I don't appreciate you manipulating me this way."

"I had no choice."

Dad put his hand up. "Stop while you're ahead. If you'll stick to your promise and not run away or argue anymore, I'll take you out. Better with me than by yourself."

"For sure! Way better with you, Dad." Desperate times called for extreme suck-up measures.

"Last time. Deal?" He extended a hand. "And not one more word of this after."

"YES!" I gripped his hand, and we shook on it.

"Don't ever scare us like that again, you hear? I'll call and make arrangements with Max. See if he's available this afternoon." He looked up at the graying clouds gathering above us. "Looks like rain coming."

"No. No. No. Not Max. No way. You and me. Please. This is the time we're going to find it. For real."

Dad shot me a warning look. "No can do." He craned his neck to check out the sky again. "Maybe we should come back this weekend anyways. Not much sense going out if it rains."

"Only slightly overcast. No storms with lightning coming. Promise. I checked the weather app on the bus." I showed him the forecast on my phone. "And think of the benefits. Harder to get sunburned on a cloudy day."

Dad creased his forehead. "Against my better

judgment, but I'm going to roll with it, as you like to say. As long as you don't complain about Max anymore."

The dive might be up to fifty feet deep—no chance I'd ever convince Dad to dump him.

"Okay," I said.

"And I have one more requirement before you go." He handed my phone back to me.

Uh-oh. I knew what was coming.

"Call your mother."

If ever there was a worse punishment, I couldn't think of it.

18
CITY OF WASHINGTON

We stopped at the marina for gas on our way from Abuelo's dock, but when we made our way out to open water on the boat—no shocker—there was no seaweed road to lead us to gold. No magical path to follow. Even I knew better than to expect it. Instead, I had armed myself with GPS coordinates to Elbow Reef: 25 08.61N 080 15.44W. Magical numbers to the score!

After all, this was a registered dive site east of the famous John Pennekamp Coral Reef State Park. It was almost a miracle the armies of tourists we passed on the snorkeling boats near Key Largo had never marched across the hidden treasure spot. At least, I hoped . . .

I had the special goods, Great-Grandpapa's secret map locked in my brain where no one else could find it. Two hundred twenty-two steps from the wreck to the X that marks the spot.

After navigating six miles offshore, the light tower I saw in the dream rose into view. I slowed the boat to a crawl. My heart went the opposite speed—accelerating to maximum. We were close.

The mooring buoys marking the reef appeared next. Phew. We were the only boat venturing out this far, thanks be to rain. This was a protected sanctuary preservation area, so the large floating balls offered the only option to tie up. We couldn't drop anchor, or we'd risk hurting the delicate coral. Not something to mess with.

Max leaned over and grabbed hold of the rope hanging off the buoy as we drifted up to it. The waves rocked the boat out of reach, so it took him three tries to tie up. "Whew," he grunted. "This here's one of the dives where you get the rougher Gulf Stream current coming through. Kind of like Carysfort Reef, except deeper. Maybe more challenging than you're used to."

"Is it safe?" Dad's face had already turned a light shade of green from the choppy water.

"I'll take good care of Fin. Don't you worry." Max fastened us to the buoy with a bowline knot to secure our position.

Wish I could skip the worry. I still had to figure out how to grab the loot with Max on my tail, but it was go-time. I'd have to figure it out on the fly. Roll with it. Hee-hee.

Majestic angelfish in shades of blue and gold greeted us as we reached the ocean bottom. They darted in and out of a patchwork of branches—trees of the sea—towering structures of staghorn coral spiking up like antlers of a macho deer.

Farther away, on a sandy clearing of nothingness, a lone stingray skirted along. I envied him as he glided out of sight. All on his own.

Max pointed as we passed a giant loggerhead turtle over three feet in length. Not often you got up close and personal with one of these swimming right next to you, so this was a big treat for sure. This species was part of the Cheloniidae family—tough word to spell—and the largest hard-shelled type in the world. My science teacher would be real proud I retained one of her random factoids. She had us clapping out the four syllables like we were back in kindergarten, though I gotta say, it did make it easier to remember.

The wreckage from the *City of Washington* came into view next. I fought to keep my breathing steady as I examined the guts of the old ship. Purple sea fans attached to the metal carcass waved gracefully in the gentle flow of current. It was torn to pieces. Decayed. Steel beams lay scattered across the ocean floor same as bones in a ghostly graveyard. Same as the sailors who must've been on board. And same as the souls aboard the train.

The sea took its prisoners, Abuelo always said, just as it took the man holding on to the treasure. An unsettled feeling swirled around me. I could almost feel his presence close by.

I'd need to start counting steps, though way harder to swim and count footsteps instead of keeping count while skipping along a golden seaweed road. I did the mental math. One webbed fin foot would equal two of my size-seven steps. Yeah, that would do. Divide by two and I only had one hundred eleven to deal with. Easy peasy.

One. Two. Three. Four . . . I marked them off in my mind. By the time I reached fifty, the light streaming down from the surface became less intense. We were going deeper. Things were getting creepier. A lime-green moray eel popped its head out of a small underwater cave, right next to a patch of black pointy sea urchins.

Max jerked me back with a forceful tug.

Ah! My scream got sucked in the regulator.

Was Max trying to turn on me? In the shadowy depths where no one could see or hear?

A barracuda, long, silvery, and thin, bearing sharp pointy fangs, darted out from the cannon right next to me. The cannon from my dream.

Oops. I was letting my imagination get the better of me. Max was not out to harm me. He was helping. For once, I was a teeny bit grateful to have him by my side, though it was the worst possible moment to dwell on this.

I shot ahead, still measuring my steps, till a dark presence parked its body a car's length in front of me. It stared me down with one menacing eye—the other hidden on the opposite side of its head. Monocular vision. I knew animals often had this kind of sight.

This type of fish, the king predator of the seas, did. No denying it.

This could only be a . . .

SHARK!

Blacktip. Not friendly.

It circled, challenging me to take another step.

In a stealth move, I tucked in the jagged tooth

necklace underneath my rash guard. Not a good idea to leave it hanging on display, like, "Yo, buddy, got one of your cousin's teeth hanging on my neck." No way.

Next, I . . .

F-R-O-Z-E.

Still as a corpse. Meanwhile, the *Jaws* theme song drummed a mad beat in my mind.

Duunnnn . . . dunnnn . . . duuunnnn . . . dunnnn . . . duuunnnn . . . dunnnn.

He toyed with me swimming back and forth. Back and forth, to the rhythm of my drums, till finally, an object hidden beneath his shadow came into sight.

Another piece of railroad track.

Next to it lay . . . a rectangular shape, half buried in the sand. The trunk.

The treasure trunk!

YAHOO!

I screamed into the regulator. A surge of bubbles escaped above my head. I pinched myself to make sure it wasn't a dream this time.

But no, it was real. I'd found the treasure. Abuelo's treasure.

The only problem was, it came with its own deadly pirate guarding it.

Where were the nice dolphins forming the arc by the X from my dream? In real life, I got a shark instead.

Plus there was Max to deal with. I couldn't inspect my find with my babysitter on my tail.

Time to roll with it . . .

I swam back ten feet, with a school of yellowtails encircling, unaware they could be tasty snacks just like me. Max appeared at my side and signaled "up."

"Going back to the boat," I said when his head bobbed up on the surface next to me. The rain had slowed to a trickle at this point.

"You're done? Still got almost your full tank of air left. Pretty interesting stuff down here. Did you see the blacktip shark?"

Shoot. He could've stolen a glimpse of the treasure, too.

"Don't tell Dad about the shark. Please. He'll freak."

Max nodded before I left him in my wake, kicking and paddling, fast as my arms and legs could propel me.

"Back so soon?" Dad peered over the side when I approached.

I checked to make sure the coast was clear before answering. "Found it," I whispered.

"Found what?"

"What do you think, Dad?"

He looked puzzled. "The treasure? Are you kidding?"

"Shhh . . . Max is close by. I told you I would."

"Hard to believe. Impossible, in fact. It's real? Are you bringing it up?"

"Problem is, it's down about forty feet. Can't do it alone. It'll be heavy, but the water will make the trunk more buoyant. I need you to help lift it from one of the ends. We can ditch Max and come back."

"You're expecting me to go down?" Dad shot me his "are you crazy" expression again.

Ha. And I'd even left out the part about the shark. I'd never get him to go if I told him his greatest fear in the ocean lurked beneath us.

But I could try and guilt him . . . "Come on. You can't let me down now. Disappoint Abuelo and Great-Grandpapa. We've come this far. Where's your *semper fortis?*"

"My what?"

"It's a phrase Abuelo taught me from the Navy. Means courage."

"That's swell, but you know I'm not going down. Are you trying to kill me?"

"It'll be a quick plunge. Little risk." Guilt pricked at

me. A tiny needle stab at my side for telling the little white lie. "I'll teach you. Nothing to it."

"Son, I can't. Wish I could help, but I simply can't. As it is, the rocking out here with this weather already has me feeling quite sick. Let's just say, I already fed the fish."

No lie on his part. His face did look greener than before.

"You're going to have to rely on Max if you want to haul it up. I'm truly sorry."

"But how can I trust him? This is our family secret. I made a promise to Abuelo."

"You've got to lose your paranoia. I'm paying him to help you, and he's been nothing but nice to you. Professional."

He had saved me from the fangs of the giant barracuda. That had to count for something.

Max surfaced next to me. "Ready to lose the tank?"

I stared over the horizon. Down with him or out? Now or possibly never? The choice was mine.

"Well?" he prodded.

"No. Going back. Need to pick up something."

"Let me guess. For science class?"

Something about his tone made my skin crawl. But it

wasn't much of a choice to quit and leave the family legacy behind. "I found something. Need your help bringing it up."

"What is it?" he blurted.

I stayed silent. The overeagerness in his voice wasn't jiving.

"Sorry. Guess it's none of my business."

No, it's not! I wanted to scream, but instead, I laid on my best acting skills. "Old junk. My grandfather lost a suitcase full of Cuban memories, and I've been looking for it."

Doubt was obvious on Max's face. "What about the . . . you know what," he whispered.

"Dad, pass me Abuelo's speargun. Saw a big juicy fish I might hunt down for dinner."

Dad gave me a questioning look but handed over the weapon.

"Okay, then," Max said. "Right behind you."

No one or nothing was messing with me. I dove down, spear pointed in front. Ready on the attack.

19
PANTS ON FIRE

The shark was long gone when we returned to the spot. Max's eyes went wide when I pointed out the trunk. With only a little bit of digging, we were able to free it from its underwater prison.

Next we wrapped the line from the boat around the center of the trunk. I figured the handle would be corroded and flimsy after all this time, so this would help secure the case shut and give Dad something to grab on to when we got to the surface.

Max shot me a thumbs-up and we began swimming toward the light, with Max and me each supporting my find from either side. As the trunk rose, I thought about how heavy it was and how it must have dragged its original owner down like an anchor.

In minutes we broke the surface near the boat.

Wide-eyed, Dad reached down with a boat hook to grab on. Together, the three of us muscled it out of the water and onto the boat. Then we climbed up the ladder. Max matched my rush tearing off gear. He peeled off his skin-tight wetsuit, flexing his muscular build in a Speedo-type bathing suit similar to the one I'd use for swim practice, before stepping into a pair of dry boardshorts and slipping on a T-shirt. I hadn't bothered with a wetsuit and opted for drip-dry. I had more important things to worry about.

For a few minutes, we stood in the stern of the boat and just stared at the trunk in silence. Water leaked out and pooled at our feet.

"Wow!" Max finally said as he knelt down next to me to study the object. The rectangular metal case, the deepest color of rust, measured about twenty-four inches across. Spiky barnacles clung to the trunk. One of the two latches was missing, but the lock in the middle still seemed secure. "Only junk in here, aye?"

"I told you. Old family stuff. Remember when you said it was none of your business." I did my best to sound polite.

"Let's head home," Dad said. Worry marks blended in with the green still left on his face. Maybe he was beginning to see the problem with having a babysitter with us today.

Max's smile turned menacing. Worse than the shark's toothy grin. In fact, Jaws turned out to be harmless—off after an easier meal when we invaded his territory. No fight. No square off. Almost disappointing.

"What if I want to make it my business? You're hiding something from me, boy. You and your landlubber dad. Always knew that bum Kiki was up to something—playing it off like he was just a lone diver out for pleasure. But he was always checking out bizarre places where there was nothing to see. I suspected he was after something. Figured it out for sure when you and he went out diving so soon after the hurricane."

My heart hammered in my chest. I was certain Max would hear the frantic rhythm pounding against the thin fabric of my rash guard. I fought to control my voice and sound casual. "Boring antiques. That's all."

"I love antiques," Max said. He pulled the case closer to him. "How about I steal a peek?"

"No," Dad said, jumping between us. "Step back, Max. We're not paying you to take a look."

I gaped. Dad sounded as hard-nosed as a drill sergeant.

"You going to arrest me?" Max mocked. He raised his hands in the air.

The next second, he sprang into motion and grabbed the fishing spear off the deck. He aimed the three barbed points at Dad's heart. "Don't move an inch. I don't want to hurt you or your son."

Dad stood tall, not a tremble to be seen. I couldn't figure out how he'd be afraid to go in the water but not freak out with a nasty weapon aimed at his chest.

He looked Max straight in the eyes. "How do you think you're going to get away with this? When we get back to shore, I'm going to have to report you."

Max laughed.

Ugh. Dad's cool drill-sergeant vibe evaporated. Why'd he have to go there?

As Max turned his attention back on the trunk, I stared at Dad and tried to send him brain waves: No more talking!

Dad's pupils expanded when it was clear he got the message. Because duh, at this point there was only one thing Max was going to do when he got a look inside the trunk.

Gulp. We were goners for sure.

I had to do something.

With the point of the pole still threatening Dad, Max bent over and retrieved a short diving knife from his duffel. Turning his body half-around and shifting the spear to his left hand, he wrenched the knife into the trunk's lock with his right.

He took his eyes off Dad to examine the latch mechanism, and in that very second, Dad leaped forward.

Clonk! He knocked the spear out of Max's left hand.

My mouth dropped open watching superhero Dad come to life.

Go, Dad, go!

But, oh no. Max slashed backward with the knife, gashing Dad at the waist.

Blood seeped over Dad's shirt, staining the tacky yellow pineapple pattern of his favorite drugstore tourist shirt.

I moved to help.

"I'm okay, Fin," he said, but his eyes told a different story as he retreated to the bow of the Whaler and crouched like a wounded animal. Blood dripped from his wound, bright red against the white deck.

"Stand back," Max snarled. He pointed the blade of

his knife at me this time. "If you behave, I won't need to hurt you, too."

My feet stayed glued, but I had to help Dad. I tore off my rash guard and threw it in his direction. "Use this. Put pressure on the wound." I'd done this myself when I cut my hand on the railroad track.

Max growled and shifted his attention back to the lock.

This was my only chance.

I inched my way back toward the storage compartment in the console underneath the steering wheel. There had to be something I could use. Anything to serve as protection.

Dad's giant first-aid kit mocked me, lying on the floor. I could use it to help Dad, but it wouldn't be of much use otherwise. Couldn't exactly gauze up Max's hands together.

Bright orange plastic peeked out between other tools inside the compartment. I picked out the colored piece by the handle, hiding it behind my back. Not sure how it'd match up to a knife, but it could buy us time.

"Got it!" Max exclaimed, breaking apart the lock. He propped the trunk open.

A tomb-like silence fell over the three of us as we

stood and gaped at the contents. It was one thing to dream about treasure, another to see it in real life. It was hard to believe this trunk was filled with hundreds of coins. The case didn't look like a pirate's chest, but the contents came close.

Max's eyes bulged out of their sockets. "Family junk, aye? Enough gold here to buy me a private island."

He placed the bloodstained knife on top of the pile of coins, grabbing armfuls and tossing them in the air. "I finally got my payday," he said. Then he giggled. Yes, he actually giggled.

"It's not yours! Step away," I commanded.

Max picked up the knife again and whipped around to face me. His eyes blazed maniacally. "What are you going to do about it?"

"This." I swung around the orange flare gun and faced it at him. "Don't make me shoot."

Max laughed again, holding his stomach for extra emphasis. "You think you're going to stop me with that?" He lunged.

My finger pulled back on the trigger.

Pa-POP!

The noise came louder than expected. The sound of a firecracker exploding—firing off the distress signal.

Along with the pop, a small burst of flame shot out from the barrel, as the flare whizzed out across the water.

If Max had stayed put, he would have been fine, and I would have been toast. But because he lunged toward me, the flame from the barrel caught the edge of his shorts on fire. "Ay! Ay! Ay!" Max screamed, jumping up and down on one leg.

"Liar, liar, pants on fire!" I taunted. I was done with his lies and with him pretending to be good. Besides, I'd never forgive him for hurting Dad.

He slapped at his bathing suit to put out the blaze.

"Jump in the water! It's the only way to put out the fire!"

"And let you have the treasure? No way!" he screamed.

"I'd jump in if I were you. Before the fire spreads to your privates."

Max looked down at his shorts and crossed his hands over the midsection. But the flames seemed to grow and in a second or two he leaped for it.

Splash!

His body hit the ocean, squelching the fire.

Before he could swim back to the boat I rushed to turn on the motor.

Max popped his head out of the water, arms flailing high above. "You can't leave me here!"

"Fin." Dad hobbled over to my side, clutching a hand over his bloodstained waist. "Wait. He could drown."

"Doubt it, but here . . ." I yanked open the storage seat and pulled out an orange life jacket matching the color of the flare gun, along with a ring buoy. After tossing them to where Max was treading water, I propelled the boat forward.

After gunning it for a hundred yards or so, I slammed the throttle back to idle.

"What are you doing now?" Dad asked as I was getting the GPS coordinates on my navigating app on my phone.

"Making sure my evil babysitter gets rescued—by the right people. I need to get us out of here. Get you to a doctor."

I grabbed the radio and put out a Mayday call to the Coast Guard. When I had raised them on the radio, I told them about the man overboard and gave them the coordinates to Elbow Reef. After we got that sorted out, I also told them my father had been stabbed by the man in the water. That prompted a burst of new questions.

Dad hobbled over and sat down next to me in the captain's chair. He grabbed the mic from me and said he would take over from here. As he started telling the operator what had happened, he looked at me and pointed straight ahead. I knew what he meant:

Get us to Abuelo's. As soon as possible.

As I throttled up I thought of something.

Dad and I made a pretty great team.

20
CSI

Dad's face had turned pale by the time we reached Abuelo's dock. This time it wasn't the sunscreen turning him white.

Before hopping off the boat and tying us up, I hid the trunk under a bunch of towels. "Wait here. I'm going to see if Captain Pete's home and ask him to drive us to the medical clinic up at the strip mall next to the drugstore. You okay if I leave you alone for a minute?"

"Don't worry. It's not as bad as it looks," Dad said. "Hand me the first-aid box and I'll see if I can clean this up. Never thought I'd be using the kit on myself."

When I returned with Captain Pete, Dad had wrapped bandages round and round his waist, so his midsection looked like a mummy's.

"Nasty splinter there, eh?" Captain Pete asked.

"Little mishap with the fish spear," Dad said, mustering a half-smile.

"Getting into trouble like your old man, I see." Captain Pete stepped on board and propped Dad up against him. Between the two of us, we carried him off the boat.

"Real sorry to impose on you." Dad winced, clutching his side.

"Nonsense, we fishermen help each other out." Captain Pete winked.

Sixteen stitches and sixty minutes later, we returned from the clinic. When Captain Pete dropped us off, a police car waited in Abuelo's driveway, parked tail-first between Max's and Abuelo's pickups.

The cop got out and slammed his door shut as we approached. Sweat dripped down his face and left marks under his armpits.

"Officer Martinez." He extended a hand after showing Dad his badge. "Mind if I ask you a few questions?"

"Of course not, come inside." Dad escorted him in and offered a seat. "You look like you need to cool off."

"Sure do, lousy AC in my cruiser is on the fritz."

"Fin, why don't you grab the officer a glass of water?"

"Much appreciated, young man." Officer Martinez wriggled his bulky frame onto an armchair.

Long minutes later, I returned with a bottle of spring water. "Sorry. Seems a crime to use plastic by the ocean, but I know we still have the boil water order from the hurricane. This one's fresh from our cooler out back."

I settled into the sofa next to Dad ready to help him face the inquisition. Reminded me of when I got sent to the principal's office last year at school when I got in trouble for goofing off in—yeah, you guessed it—science class. Lots of explaining to do. My stomach filled with mosquitoes, this time attacking from the inside.

"I'm sure you know why I'm here." Officer Martinez pulled out a small notepad and pencil. "We already had an interesting chat with Max Tinkler. Got him with us in custody after the Coast Guard rescued him. Heard you called it in but left him floating in open water and told the Coast Guard quite a story."

I jumped in. "He . . . he tried to kill my dad. I was scared. We had to get away from him."

"That's his car outside next to mine?" Officer Martinez asked though it was more of a statement. It was clear he already knew the answer.

"Let me explain," Dad said, taking over. "I just returned from the clinic, as you can see. Sixteen stitches." He patted the bandage at his waist and his face flinched with a slightly dramatic touch of agony.

Hee-hee. Bravo!

"Max stabbed me and could've killed us both. He deserves to be in jail."

Officer Martinez studied Dad's face. "Do you know what provoked his behavior?"

Dad took his time to answer. "I'm not sure what makes a man lose control like that. What did Max have to say for himself? I hired the man to escort my son diving. He turned on us out there."

"What do you mean he turned on you? Can you be more specific?" Officer Martinez urged.

"He wanted our money," I said, which was one hundred percent true. "He's a thief. A bad person," I offered. "All I know is he would have killed us."

Officer Martinez flicked his pencil against his notepad. Tap. Tap. Tap. "Mr. Tinkler claims you shot him with a flare gun." He directed his comment at me.

Now it was my turn to get dramatic. I started blubbering, and the tears came pouring out.

"Wait a minute." Dad raised his voice. "My son was

defending me. I was hurt. Bleeding. You see." He pointed out his bandage again. "Max lunged at my son with a knife, and the flare gun went off. If he hadn't been so close, his pants wouldn't have caught on fire."

"Yes, I can see you got hurt. I'm going to need you to come down to the station later and make a full statement." Officer Martinez stood up. "Is your boat docked out back?"

Dad nodded.

"Mind if I take a look?"

Dad's eyes got all shifty, making it obvious he was clawing his brain for an excuse. "It's filthy. Covered in my blood. Haven't had a chance to clean it yet," he finally said.

"Exactly how I want it. It's the crime scene."

"Are you saying we've committed a crime?" Dad said.

"It's okay." I stood up. "I'll show Officer Martinez the boat. Dad, you stay and rest here."

"But, but . . ."

"It's fine, Dad. Rest."

"No, I'm going, too." He jumped up and trailed after us.

Officer Martinez climbed aboard the *Sirena*, rocking it with his weight. His big, clunky work boots left dark tracks I'd be scrubbing, along with dried blood, for days.

Dad shot me an I'm-freaking-out look and mouthed: *the treasure.*

I answered with a thumbs-up sign.

"Mind if I collect a sample?" Officer Martinez knelt before we could respond. He rubbed a swab stick over one of the red stains splotched over the deck and zipped it into a plastic bag. "Where exactly were you standing when Max Tinkler allegedly attacked?"

"I'll show you." I leaped on board and moved to the exact position where Max stabbed Dad. "Knife to Dad's gut." I rolled my eyes back for effect. "Then"—I moved to the front—"I reached in here, grabbed the flare gun to defend us, and fired when Max tried to get me." I ended with more dramatic flair, fake shot to the air.

"It's the only thing I could find for protection. Blood was gushing out of my dad, and I got real scared." I finished my performance with a hint of more blubbering, holding back a bow.

"It's okay, son." Officer Martinez nodded. "You were lucky to get away."

"Is this all the information you need?" Dad asked, coming aboard as well. "Quite the long day. We could both use some rest."

"I understand." Officer Martinez continued to scan the boat with his eyes. "Mind if I look under here?" He moved toward the pile of towels.

I could tell Dad was thinking of falling overboard or staging some other distraction. "Yes—"

"Of course not," I said, shooting Dad a warning glance.

Dad answered with frantic eyes as I shook my head. He held his breath as Officer Martinez lifted the towels.

"Fin," the officer said, raising a flipper.

I looked over at my dad with a smile and he rolled his eyes.

"Okay, I've seen enough. I'll let you two be." He stepped back onto the dock. "I may need to return if anything else develops. And we'll need you to come by to make a formal statement."

Dad exhaled and we followed Officer Martinez inside. "What about Max's car? It's still parked outside."

"We'll take care of it. I'll send someone to remove it from your property tonight."

"Is Max in jail?" I blurted. "You said you had him in

custody, but will he be released? He could come after us."

"Don't worry yourself for now. I'm pretty sure he'll be locked up for a while. He's on parole and should not have had a weapon in his possession, for starters. And today's incident isn't looking good for him."

"I interviewed Max before I hired him." Dad frowned. "Should have done a thorough background check." He shook his head and walked Officer Martinez to the door.

Violet-scented air wafted in when it swung open. Mami stood on the doormat with a wriggly Ratón in her arms.

"Hello!" she squealed, before embracing Dad and leaving a red lipstick stain on his cheek. "Are you all right? I drove down, fast as I could, when you called from the hospital."

"Clinic." Dad flinched. "A little sore."

She wrapped me in a hug next. "*Y mi amor.* You gave us such a scare this morning."

Mami noticed Officer Martinez for the first time. "Good evening, sir. Not too fast, of course. I didn't drive fast at all."

"I'm sure." Officer Martinez gave Mami an appreciative nod. "You folks have a good night." He walked out and we watched him squeeze into his car, nestled between Max's and Abuelo's pickups.

When he backed out, the logo on the side of Max's truck became visible. CONCHER SCUBA with the bottom of the big *C* snaking under the other letters. The lightbulb turned on in my head. I'd seen this logo when I dove with Abuelo right before the hurricane, back before his stroke. I should have picked up on this clue. This may have even been the sea serpent that crashed my dream—not Sly's tattooed one. Max had been scoping out Abuelo's moves right from the start.

"Fin. Fin. You get lost again?" Dad waved his hand in front of my face. "Where did the treasure go? That was quite a stunt you pulled on Officer Martinez."

Mami gave me a strange look. "You pulled a stunt on a police officer, young man?"

"We may have lied a little," Dad admitted.

Before Mami could respond I assured them both. "We never lied, Dad. We simply left out a few details."

"*Oye*, wait!" Mami's face registered serious excitement. "Did you just say 'treasure'? You actually found it? The treasure exists? Why didn't you tell me when you called? *¡Que emoción!*"

"The treasure is safe and sound. Thanks to Dad."

"Thanks to me? What do you mean?"

"I was real happy to get the nice police officer water when you asked. Didn't you notice I was gone for a while? Took me a bit to lug the trunk onto Abuelo's wheelbarrow on my own."

Mami clapped her hands together. "I'm totally lost. You boys have a lot of explaining to do."

Dad grinned from ear to ear. "Coconspirators," he whispered in my ear, for once burying all his hang-ups.

"Yes." I winked, or did my eye spasm blinking thing. Like Abuelo and me.

And then I took a deep breath and told Mami what had happened.

21
SPOOK THE LOOT

When I finished talking, Mami was shaking her head in disbelief. And smiling. *"Nuestro héroe,"* she said. And then she laughed. "Fin, *mi amor*, you got so caught up telling me the story, you haven't even shown me the treasure yet. Women love sparkly things. Show me the gold!"

"Way to a woman's heart." Dad winked. "Gold and big sparkly diamonds."

Mami batted her eyes and blew him a kiss.

Gross.

"Follow me to my lair." I laughed. "Also known as Abuelo's shed."

The oversized storage room, built of concrete to fight off the elements, was crammed with all sorts of outdoor equipment to entertain. Hours of fun in the sun. Besides the row of fishing rods lining the walls, there were kayaks, tubes, old rafts, nets, and of course, lots of dive gear.

"This place is a mess. Perhaps our next father-son project should be organizing this shed." Dad peeked inside but remained standing behind the double entry doors.

"Abuelo would have a fit!" I laughed. "He likes it just the way it is, and so do I. Perfectly filled with all our favorite toys. And now for the coolest thing of all. Dear Mami, I present to you, the TREASURE!"

Mami gasped when I sprang open the lid of the trunk. "*¡Dios mío!* So many coins. I can't believe this is even real."

"First time I get a close-up look." Dad scooted in next to Mami. "Couldn't see much with Max blocking. There's an inscription on the inside of the trunk. Let me get my glasses."

"I can read it." I grabbed a flashlight off a shelf and leaned in. "It's faded, but there's a name: Harold Pickerberry."

"Must be the owner." Dad scratched his head. "The man who perished on the train."

A gust of wind rattled the door to the shed, bringing with it a sudden dip in temperature along with the salty smell of ocean. The hair on the back of my neck stood at high alert, and the same unsettled feeling I'd felt down in the depths wrapped around me with a cold embrace.

Mami gave me a worried look. It was obvious she sensed something, too. "Mr. Pickerberry's spirit is not at peace," she whispered.

"What are you two talking about?" asked Dad.

"We're not alone," I said in a spooky voice.

"Not funny." Dad shook his head. "No such thing as ghosts."

"True . . . but maybe there's more to the story. Something else we're supposed to figure out." I clawed at the corners of my brain to remember something Great-Grandpapa said to me in the dream—right before Mami woke me.

"I think we need to talk about what comes next," she said. "And your father needs to rest."

The next morning, before dawn, we began loading Dad's car. If any neighbors happened to be watching, they may have wondered why I was rolling a wheelbarrow out from the shed and loading what looked like a big plastic bag of garbage into the trunk of the car.

"Hurry up if you still plan to follow us, dear," Dad called out to Mami.

"*Pero, mi cara.* I haven't put my face on."

"What's wrong with the one you have?" Dad teased. "I've loved it for sixteen years."

Mami gave Dad a swat. "Just give me a few more minutes, silly."

Fifteen minutes later we were ready to go. As we locked the front door, Captain Pete stepped out of his house and squatted to grab a newspaper off his lawn. "Heading back so early?"

"Work," Dad responded.

"And school!" Mami added, although we were doing neither of those things.

Once Dad and I were underway, with Mami following right behind, I burst out laughing.

"What's so funny?" he asked.

"Now we're all conspirators!"

22
PIRATE BOOTY

We drove straight to Abuelo's facility. I ran in to grab a wheelchair from the reception area and borrowed a folded bedsheet from a housekeeping cart so it wouldn't look like I had a cadaver stashed in a black garbage bag.

Minutes later, we were rolling the chair back toward Room 222 with the treasure trunk on the seat, hidden under the white sheet.

"What have you got there?" asked a young perky attendant at the nurses' station. "A ghost?"

A nervous laugh escaped. She wasn't far off from the truth. "Some family heirlooms to brighten my abuelo's day!" I said.

"Perfect timing. Mr. Roman's awake and watching TV, but I think he could use some cheering up."

"Great. And it's Román," Mami muttered under her breath as we followed the nurse.

Abuelo's shades were open this time when we entered. Sunlight streamed in, illuminating his face in the bed.

The nurse gave us a lopsided smile. "Oopsie. Seems he dozed off."

I flicked on the overhead lights before I rushed to his side. "I'll get him to wake—

"Abuelo," I yelled. "I've got the best news!"

His eyes fluttered gently like butterfly wings before they propped open.

"There you go. Super!" The nurse grinned. "I'll give you all some privacy." She stepped out.

Abuelo looked at me with the same blank stare I'd seen before.

"Did you hear me?" I said. "Good news."

"Not my hearing that's messed up," he snapped. "But nothing to wake up for these days." He shook his head and grunted. His voice strained as though it wasn't getting much use. "Might as well stick me in a coffin already if I'm going to be stuck in this square box of a room."

"*¡Ay, por Dios!*" Mami wagged her finger. "Don't talk this way."

"Fin's got something to brighten your day," Dad interrupted.

"You're scattering my ashes at sea?" Abuelo looked hopeful.

"Not happening anytime soon," Dad chided.

I knew I had the right medicine. The cure. "We found it!" I blurted.

"Found what?" He yawned. "My Jell-O? Been waiting for it to arrive. Only good thing around here. Cherry flavor. My favorite."

"The treasure, Abuelo."

"I get it . . . you sneaked in a *cafecito*?" He gave Mami a hopeful look, searching her hands for a clue. "Better score than even the Jell-O. Been cut off from caffeine since I got thrown in this jail."

"Abuelo. It's not coffee. I mean the real treasure."

"What are you going on about, boy?"

"Your treasure! From the train."

Abuelo's face perked up. "Huh?" His eyebrows furrowed. "You're not pulling my leg, are you?"

"For real." Mami and I stepped out of the way, and Dad rolled the chair forward with the treasure chest, popping open the top so the gold glinted.

Abuelo's jaw dropped, and he sat straight up in bed. He opened his mouth to speak and closed it again. Opened. Closed.

"Got anything to say?" Dad teased.

"I wasn't about to let you down. Let Great-Grandpapa down," I said, and grabbed a handful of coins out of the trunk, handing them to Abuelo.

Still silent, his face registered shock. He took his time examining the gold and rubbing his fingers over the shiny surface of one of the coins. It was round and worn with uneven edges and bore the symbol of a square cross.

Abuelo's eyes turned misty before he found his voice. "Spanish gold. Traveled from Spain to Cuba and now here. This is an escudo piece, otherwise known as a doubloon." He turned it over. "See the crest on this side, *el escudo*. Probably dates back to the sixteenth century."

"Pirate treasure! Like you said it would be. We have the coolest heritage."

"Don't you forget it." Mami smiled.

"Always be proud of your beans," Abuelo agreed.

"His beans?" Mami tilted her head.

"Don't worry, I threw your Puerto Rican *habichuelas* into the Caribbean mix."

"Dad and I didn't do so bad. We found it together."

"Now that'd be something to see." He chuckled. "Victor helped?"

"You should have seen Dad. He got stabbed and everything. *Semper fortis* to the Max." Hee-hee. "Get it, Dad?"

"Stabbed, you say?" Abuelo raised an eyebrow.

"By a pirate."

"Hmm, tell me more." He rubbed his hands together. "This is starting to sound like a real adventure."

I told Abuelo about running away, Dad finding me, and our last-chance adventure on the boat. When we got to the fight scene, he held up his hand.

"Max? You mean Max Tinkler of Concher Scuba?"

"I know, right?" I rolled my eyes. "Like we needed a babysitter."

"Max told me he knew you," Dad said, ignoring my comment. "One of the reasons I hired him."

"Hmph. No wonder he turned up in a lot of places I dove. Must've been tracking me for years."

"I agree. He was after you from the start. I saw the logo on his pickup and recognized it from the boat we saw the time we were diving right before the hurricane. Trouble is, figured it out too late. It should've been a clue."

Dad chewed on his lip. "Seems I'm the one to blame.

Max approached me the first time we were out on your *Sirena*. Must've recognized the boat. Fin and Sly were down beneath the surface. He introduced himself. Said he ran one of the best scuba operations."

"Don't beat yourself up," Abuelo said. "Won't do us any good. *Carpe diem*, remember? Focus on today."

"Yes! The best day." I punched the air.

"Still can't believe you found it after all these years. You haven't answered the million-dollar question, though. No pun intended." He chuckled. "Where? Where the heck did you find it? I must've searched hundreds of spots throughout the years."

"Near Elbow Reef."

"That's far from where it got swept out. How'd you ever figure out to look there? I sure didn't leave you any good clues."

"Got hold of the treasure map. Great-Grandpapa gave it to me in a dream."

"You mean my papá?" Abuelo's gaze drifted to a far-away place. "I've had all sorts of dreams with him lately. Crazy stuff."

"Trust me. My dream was totally cuckoo. Let's just say I practically visited the Land of Oz with an evil sea serpent chasing me."

Mami's eyes widened. "*Pobrecito*. Sounds awful. You never told me all the details."

"There's something we want to ask you." Dad interrupted Mami's pity fest. He poked me to take the lead.

Gulp. Here goes . . . "Abuelo, I've been thinking, and I want to ask you something. Because it's your treasure. I found it for you. And you searched your whole life for it."

"Go on." A sparkle returned to Abuelo's eyes.

"We found the owner's name branded inside the trunk: Harold Pickerberry." I pointed it out so Abuelo could see for himself. "You mentioned he died at sea trying to protect the treasure—got swept out holding on."

"That's right. It killed my papá that he couldn't save him. A heavy burden he carried."

The ceiling lights flickered on and off, and I got the same tickle I'd felt on the back of my neck in Abuelo's shed the night before. There was one big difference. It didn't feel at all creepy this time. No. It was more of a love tickle.

Abuelo stared at the ceiling and a slight grin marked his face.

I could tell Mami felt something unusual, too. Discreetly, she made the sign of the cross.

I continued. "It's kind of my point. Last night I was able to track the Pickerberry family down with Google."

"You see, Pickerberry is a rather unique name," Dad chimed in. "We discovered he left behind a wife and a baby son when he died. The family established themselves in the Lower Keys."

"Old conchs," I added. "Living in Key West their entire lives."

"His son died a few years ago," Dad continued, "but he's got a granddaughter and grandson. They run a maritime foundation, a year-round ocean studies camp. It teaches kids all about the habitat and about marine ecology and preservation. Contributes to some pretty amazing research. Or at least it did."

"What do you mean?" Abuelo asked.

"The campsite got destroyed by Hurricane Irma. It's right next to where the eye hit. Needs to be rebuilt, but insurance won't cover most of the costs. The Pickerberrys are out of money. May need to shut it down."

Abuelo stayed silent, his forehead creased.

Dad and I exchanged glances.

After a long while, Abuelo let out a long sigh. "I think I know what you want to ask, Fin, and you don't even need to."

"Doesn't seem right for us to keep it." I nodded.

"No, it's not. When did you get to be so smart? Give

the darned treasure away—back to the ocean. Back to the Keys. To the Pickleburgers—where it belongs. I'm sure Papá would want it this way."

"Pickerberry," Dad corrected him.

Realization slapped me across the face. "I couldn't remember before, but Great-Grandpapa actually told me this in my dream. He said, 'Use it to help another.' It must be what he meant. And if you don't mind . . ." I hesitated.

"What is it?" Abuelo prodded.

"I'd like to correct a wrong. I judged someone—in a bad way—and made him lose out on money. It's been bothering me. I'd like to give Slippety Sly one of the coins so he can buy a better car to ride his grandma in."

"Who is this Sly character?" Abuelo asked.

"My first babysitter," I groaned. "The good one of the two."

"Welp, can't say I saw that one coming." Dad grinned.

"It's a nice gesture." Mami smiled. She patted her heart and looked around the room. "We've got everything we need right here."

Dad gathered Mami and me into a hug. "She's right. I had my first adventure—what you've been telling me to do all my life." He smiled at Abuelo. "It was worth more than gold to connect with Fin. Stab wound and all."

I'd never understood what my special link to Cuba and the Caribbean meant, but I'd discovered my roots. My unique story.

A little bit mystery. A little bit scary. A little bit sweet. A little bit daring. And yes, even a bit annoying. All parts of me. Blood. History. Family. This was my story.

"Seems you uncovered the right kind of treasure." Abuelo stared deep into my eyes.

It could have been my imagination, but his brimmed with tears.

"Don't be getting all soft on me," Dad teased.

"Time I got out of here." Abuelo's voice returned to gruff. He yanked off a cord attached to his chest. The machine behind him responded with beeps while the squiggles on the display monitors made a mad dance across the screen. "Let's go home."

I rushed to grab Abuelo's arm, steady him as he rose.

"I can manage on my own," he snapped. His forearms swelled as he propped himself up, tall and strong.

"He's baaaack." Dad laughed.

I wrapped my arms around Abuelo. "You got any more adventures for us?"

ACKNOWLEDGMENTS

I am grateful for the treasure trove of contributors who helped bring *Treasure Tracks* into the world.

Many thanks to my amazing editor, Wesley Adams, for enthusiastically supporting my debut. You helped make this book so much better! I'd also like to give a big shout-out to the entire team at Farrar Straus Giroux/ Macmillan, including Melissa Warten, Hannah Miller, production editor Kat Kopit, and publicist Tatiana Merced-Zarou, for all your hard work. I'm enamored with the gorgeous cover designed by Trisha Previte and the illustration created by Antonio Javier Caparo, whose artistic vision brought Fin to life.

To my agent, Stephen Fraser at the Jennifer De Chiara Literary Agency—thanks for championing my work and diverse voices, making this dream come true.

I also want to thank Jeni Chapelle for a developmental edit that encouraged me to dive into a deeper point of view. And I'm grateful to count on writing friends for feedback, advice, and camaraderie, including the SCBWI Aventura critique group, Las Musas, and KidLit Latinx members. My lifelong amiga, Betty de Aragon, also helped with a beta read, and Cristina Diaz-Fullen, you inspired the inclusion of the Virgen de la Caridad del Cobre.

To my three sons—thanks for reading countless drafts and brainstorming with me every step of the way. We were quarantined in the Florida Keys when I wrote most of this novel, and writing it became a family affair. Roberto, you were instrumental in scoping out dive sites and their history. Marcos, you helped add humor and wit to the voice (and wrote the part about the squid dissection, based on your experience in fifth grade). Luke, you were a superstar giving feedback. To Robert, my husband, you were limitless with ideas and with your love and support. It was your abuelo, Rogelio Rodriguez, a train engineer in Cuba, who inspired this historical reference.

And to my mami in heaven, it was you who nurtured my love of reading and the ocean.

Mis tesoros, se los agradezco de todo corazón.

TURN THE
PAGE FOR

TREASURE
TRACKS

BONUS
MATERIALS

S. A. RODRIGUEZ

What did you want to be when you grew up?
When I was in grade school, I wanted to be a flight attendant to have the opportunity to travel all over the world. I grew up in Puerto Rico and didn't travel beyond the neighboring Caribbean islands until I was about fourteen years old. I always dreamed of visiting the US mainland and exploring faraway lands. I imagine it's why I loved to escape through books—and still do. Books can whisk you to make-believe worlds.

When did you realize you wanted to be a writer?
It was only after I left a demanding corporate career working in Hispanic and diversity marketing, where I did more serious types of writing, that I had time to pursue the fun, fictional kind of writing I do now. I started drafting novels as a hobby—a way to lose myself in imaginary worlds I created. As a mom to three Latino boys, I also realized there were few opportunities for them to see themselves represented in books. This gave me the motivation

and courage to realize I wanted to be a professional writer and contribute to diverse representation in books.

What's your most embarrassing childhood memory?

I was incredibly shy as a kid, so many things would embarrass me. I remember that any time I had to present a project to my class, I would go up to the front of the room with my face bright red, knees shaking, and voice cracking. I've since gotten over this shyness, and as an adult, enjoy presenting at school when I make author visits. I even presented to my son's entire middle school in a huge auditorium, and he couldn't believe I wasn't nervous. Neither could I . . .

What's your favorite childhood memory?

My favorite memory involves sailing. I remember looking out from the bow of my dad's sailboat and seeing endless crystalline ocean and silhouettes of mountain peaks dotting the landscape. Dolphins frolicked to our port, and the wind whipped back my hair as the boat glided along the turquoise waters surrounding the Virgin Islands, in the Caribbean. I'd never seen anything so beautiful. It was a perfect moment in time that I keep stored away when I need a mental escape.

As a young person, who did you look up to most?

I looked up to my abuelita the most. I lived with my grandparents until I was six years old, while my mom attended law school and began her professional career. I considered my grandmother to be a pioneer in her time. She was the principal of a high school in Puerto Rico and was awarded a scholarship to obtain a master's degree at Columbia University in the 1930s, a time when women did not often leave the island to obtain advanced degrees. She taught me the value of working hard and pursuing a good education.

What was your favorite thing about school?

Recess and library time were my favorites. My mom picked me up late on most days since she had a demanding career as a lawyer, so the library was my go-to place after school. I'd either volunteer to help stack books, read, or get my homework done, and as a bonus, it had the best AC (an important consideration when you live on a tropical island).

What were your hobbies as a kid? What are your hobbies now?

As a kid, I loved collecting shells. During grade school, I lived by the ocean, so I would scout the sand in the early morning to see what treasures the surf washed in overnight. To this day, I still like to collect shells and use them for crafts. I also like to dabble in drawing and painting, but only for fun. I mostly draw—you may have guessed—marine animals. My favorite sea creature to draw is an octopus, though I may take a stab at drawing a different type of cephalopod next: a squid!

Did you play sports as a kid?

The sport I enjoyed most as a kid was swimming. I swam with my school during PE class, and since I lived by the beach, I swam in the ocean for fun. I was a bit of a tomboy, and although I did not participate in organized sports teams, I did spend lots of time biking, roller-skating, and climbing trees. I remember always scraping my knees.

What was your first job, and what was your "worst" job?

My first job was working at the mall in a clothing store. I was a junior in high school at the time, and this pushed me to be less introverted. My worst job was working as an office assistant where I was designated "professional filer." I had to file papers in a back room all day with little to no human interaction. It was so boring that I could barely keep my eyes open. Working in a store and talking to strangers all day was way more fun.

What book is on your nightstand now?

I have a tall stack of books on my nightstand threatening to topple over, so it's impossible to name just one. There is a mix of middle-grade gems, including *Refugee* by Alan Gratz, one of my favorite books, which my youngest son is devouring at the moment. I also love reading books written by other Latinx authors, so *The Last Cuentista*, *Shine on, Luz Véliz!*, and *Cuba in My Pocket* are included atop my pile.

How did you celebrate publishing your first book?

My official celebration took place when I received the box of author copies and could hold *Treasure Tracks* in my hands for the first time. I unboxed the books by the ocean, where the story was inspired, along with my family. Something unexpected happened when we headed to the parking lot to leave: my eldest son was missing. I retraced my steps to the beach, only to find him on his hands and knees picking up trash. This touched my heart and was the best possible way to end my celebration, because I've raised my kids to be stewards of the sea, and themes of ocean conservancy are included in *Treasure Tracks*.

Where do you write your books?

I have a laptop that goes wherever I go, so I'll write by the ocean, my kitchen counter or dining room table, a park bench—pretty much anywhere. I do love to write outdoors when it's not too hot and the mosquitoes aren't swarming in for a score. *Treasure Tracks* was mostly written in the Florida Keys while my family was quarantined there for six months during the pandemic. I was living the inspiration.

What sparked your imagination for *Treasure Tracks*?

I've always been obsessed with treasure hunting, and I love learning about Florida's history. I'd read a book about Henry Flagler, an industrialist pioneer in Florida, and another one about his Overseas Railroad connecting Key West to the mainland. I'd learned that a powerful hurricane had destroyed the railroad, washing some of the railcars to sea. I gave a fictional twist to a real-life event by embedding a treasure in one of the lost railcars. Other books, especially nonfiction ones, can be important sources of inspiration, and this was the case for me.

What challenges do you face in the writing process, and how do you overcome them?

My biggest challenges are time management and focus. With three kids of my own, I manage a busy household and a slew of activities. As an author, I need to carve out hours of writing time and make room for promotional activities. While my kids are at school, I take advantage and do most of my writing. I also try to isolate myself from distractions since I know I have a short attention span. Social media is a big time thief, so when I'm on deadline, I turn off my phone. I also multitask "family time" by including my kids in the writing process. We brainstorm ideas together, and they are my best editors because they are brutally honest.

What is your favorite word?

Perseverance is my favorite word, and it's also a theme in all my books. I've always pushed myself to trek on even when the odds are stacked against me, and I motivate my three boys to keep going when they face challenges. One of the hardest things I've done is to break into the publishing industry and get my book out in the world. It was hard because there were so many factors outside of my control. The attitude I adopted is that I would never give up until I accomplished this goal.

Speaking of perseverance, in your author's note you spoke about living through your share of hurricanes. At the time you're answering this question, Hurricane Ian has just swept through the area. How did your lived experience influence the scenes in which Fin's family endures a similarly devasting storm?

Growing up in Puerto Rico and living in South Florida, I've coexisted with hurricanes my entire life and have learned to prepare and roll with the punches. Scenes from Hurricane Ian, which swept through the west coast of Florida, show total devastation and unspeakable loss. My experiences in general pale in comparison to the impact of this hurricane, but they did influence the scenes in the novel. For example, similar to Fin and his family, mine has spent the night in our laundry room to ensure safety, and I can vouch for the roaring noise of a hurricane sounding like a train going over the roof. Descriptions of post-hurricane damage I included, like a tree falling on the house, the pool turning into a green swamp, and losing electricity for weeks, were all influenced by things that happened to me in real life. Hurricane Irma, which is referenced in the book, was a storm that made landfall in the Florida Keys a few years back. As described in the story, I also drove down to Key Largo as soon as the roads were cleared. The damage and debris Fin describes while he makes this drive south is an almost literal account of what I witnessed.

If you could live in any fictional world, what would it be?

I'm going to go back to my youth for this answer. The fictional world I would choose to live in is Narnia. Growing up, my favorite books were The Chronicles of Narnia. I always imagined myself as Lucy, chasing adventures and battling fantastical creatures to save my kingdom.

Who is your favorite fictional character?

I also grew up reading Marvel comics, and I've watched every Marvel movie with my boys. A little-known fact is that my maiden name is Marvil (with an "i"), so I'd have to say my favorite fictional character is Captain Marvel because we (almost) share the same name and because she's one of the toughest superheroes and saves the world.

If you could travel in time, where would you go and what would you do?

If I had the opportunity to travel in time, I'd want to go back and hang with my people—the family members I have lost. I'd like to travel to Puerto Rico and spend more time with my abuelita and abuelito and meet my mom when she was in her teens. I'd also take the opportunity to meet my paternal grandfather and grandmother by traveling to 1930s Key West. Perhaps I could even meet their neighbor at the time, the famous author Ernest Hemingway. I'm sure he'd inspire some interesting stories.

My father and grandfather in Key West, c. 1930

If you could ask Ernest Hemingway one question about writing, what would it be and why?
To be honest, I'd start by asking Hemingway about his adventures and exploits around the world, including the twenty years he spent in Cuba, before I dove into the subject of writing. I find his life stories, including his passion for big-game fishing (which inspired *The Old Man and the Sea*), to be fascinating, particularly since I understand that my grandfather joined him on fishing expeditions a time or two. "Good writing is true writing," is one of Hemingway's famous writing quotes, so I think getting to know him better and learning how he was able to translate his incredible experiences into

books and write his truths would be the best starting point.

What's the best advice you have ever received about writing?

Writing advice that I love is that the revision process is what unearths the treasure. An initial draft can be messy since you are essentially telling yourself the story. With every revision round—every time you polish—you are making your story more brilliant so it can shine bright as a diamond.

What advice do you wish someone had given you when you were younger?

When I was younger, I wish I had been told to stop worrying about what others think and not measure myself against others' successes. I try to focus on this as an adult and enjoy my journey. We each have our path to follow. Fin says it best, "Plot my coordinates. Chart my destiny . . ."

Do you ever get writer's block? What do you do to get back on track?

I get writer's block, especially when I don't get enough sleep, which with three kids happens more often than I'd like. To get back on track, I read. If I'm writing and feeling less creative than usual, I also try to switch gears and focus on research. Since I often include historical elements in my novels, I find that conducting research sparks new ideas, the same as reading does. I also walk off writer's block. A walk in nature (preferably by the ocean) helps me clear my mind and get my creativity flowing.

What do you want readers to remember about your books?

I hope readers will remember how my books made them feel, and specifically as it relates to *Treasure Tracks*, I hope readers feel compelled to discover and cherish their treasures. It is also my deepest desire to have Latino kids, who may not see themselves represented in books as often, remember they deserve to be the heroes in any story.

What would you do if you ever stopped writing?

I write about adventures, but I love escaping on my own adventures and immersing myself in different cultures. If I ever stopped writing, I'd focus on family time, reading, and travel. Lots of travel. If I had the means, a dream would be to organize literacy programs for young readers in underserved communities throughout Latin America.

If you were a superhero, what would your superpower be?

My superhero alias would be Captain Marvil, pro multitasker, because my superpowers have been honed from raising three kids and doing a million things at once. I've even learned the art of writing with screaming kids and chaos all around. This is probably the reason why my books are not quiet and sometimes channel erratic energy.

Do you have any strange or funny habits? Did you when you were a kid?

A strange habit I have is that I need to put on lip gloss or lipstick every morning, even when I'm staying home by myself. And maybe . . . I'm realizing I inspired Mami's love for lipstick in *Treasure Tracks*. (Notice she's wearing lipstick to hide out in a closet at night during the hurricane scene.)

What do you consider to be your greatest accomplishment?

Without a doubt, my greatest accomplishment is raising three boys to be kind, considerate, and contributing members of society.

What would your readers be most surprised to learn about you?

Hmm . . . Maybe young readers would be surprised to learn that it's a mom writing the book and not a twelve-year-old boy, lol. When my youngest son read *Treasure Tracks*, he told me I sounded like I was his age: twelve years old. I, of course, took this as a compliment—it's more fun to be a kid. And yes, I'm quite immature and still make fart jokes.